D0065655

Evensong

Evensong

A Novel

KATE SOUTHWOOD

W. W. Norton & Company

Independent Publishers Since 1923

NEW YORK | LONDON

For information about permission to reproduce selections
from this book, write to Permissions,
W. W. Norton & Company, Inc.,
500 Fifth Avenue, New York, NY 10110

For information about special discounts for bulk purchases,
please contact W. W. Norton Special Sales at
specialsales@wwnorton.com or 800-233-4830

Manufacturing by Quad Graphics, Fairfield
Book design by Brooke Koven
Production manager: Louise Mattarelliano

Library of Congress Cataloging-in-Publication Data

Names: Southwood, Kate, author.
Title: Evensong : a novel / Kate Southwood.
Description: First edition. | New York : W. W. Norton
& Company, [2017]
Identifiers: LCCN 2016046915 | ISBN 9780393608595 (hardcover)
Classification: LCC PS3619.O9343 E94 2017 | DDC 813/.6—dc23
LC record available at https://lccn.loc.gov/2016046915

W. W. Norton & Company, Inc.
500 Fifth Avenue, New York, N.Y. 10110
www.wwnorton.com

W. W. Norton & Company Ltd.
15 Carlisle Street, London W1D 3BS

1 2 3 4 5 6 7 8 9 0

for my father

Evensong

Garfield closed the door without a sound.

Maggie Doud, he said, before he turned to face me where I stood at the foot of his bed. He'd undone his tie and top button on the way up the stairs. He came toward me then saying, A bundle of myrrh is my well-beloved unto me; he shall lie all night betwixt my breasts, and I had no more notion of whether he meant it to be sacred or profane than I knew where he'd gotten ahold of a Protestant Bible, and when I whispered, What would the priest say? he smiled a little and kept coming.

Behold, thou art fair, my love; behold, thou art fair; thou hast doves' eyes, he said, and we heard his mother clattering dishes in the sink, all the dinner dishes she had saved for this moment. He pulled his shirt free of his trousers and unbuttoned it, but I couldn't look down. He undid the top button on my blouse and the next and the next, and his voice was a whisper when he said, Behold, thou art fair, my beloved, yea, pleasant: also our bed is green. The beams of our house are cedar, and our rafters of fir.

And after, when all my clothes lay with his on the floor and I lay breathless beside him in his bed, he looked up at the ceiling and grinned.

Margaret Maguire, he said.

I wake. Joanne is watching me from over there, her face alight with helpless fury. I don't see Lee, so I close my eyes again to listen to the voices in the hall. Women's voices, but none of them Lee's. A too-loud laugh nearby, someone getting shushed, then quiet.

I move my hands till I can feel the needle in the back of my right hand, and the tape holding it there. I lift a finger to feel what I'm covered with, and it's light. Only a sheet. Little wonder I'm cold.

I want a blanket, I say.

Please, Mom, Joanne says. Don't talk.

I'm cold. I want a blanket, I say, and I hear that my voice is low and gravelly. Perhaps she can't understand me. Perhaps I need to wake up more, drink some water. I think she'd understand me fine if I said I wanted Lee, then I think better of it.

I clear my throat and that gets Joanne out of her chair, out of the room to fetch a nurse. She's afraid I'm going to keep right on talking, afraid of what I might say. I'd start by asking what she means by that look on her face and how long she plans to keep it there. How, exactly, she'd like it if I inconvenienced her further by trying to get out of this bed.

I lift the neck of the gown they've got me in and see the electrodes stuck all over my chest. I can't count them and I don't want to, either. They look like something you'd use to suck electricity out of a person to run a radio or something, and then they look more like something they'd use to pipe electricity into a body, and that's when I stop looking.

Footsteps coming, an efficient swish of pants' legs. A nurse with a smile and a blanket she's already unfolding, moving too fast for me to get in a word. She's tucked me in and even rubbed my feet through the blanket a little before Joanne is back and standing beside the bed. While the nurse is holding my wrist and looking at her watch, I look up at Joanne and purse my lips a little to tell her I know she understood me about the blanket and there's no use pretending she didn't.

The nurse is moving away already, heading for the door.

I say, Aren't you going to take these suckers off me?

Not yet, she says, holding up a finger and smiling like I'm a child she's warning away from a newly frosted cake. The doctor will be in to talk to you soon.

I know what soon means, I say when the nurse is gone. Soon means tomorrow.

Joanne doesn't say anything, and I'll grant there's nothing to say to that, so I look right at her and I try again and say, Am I too close to death to waste food on, or can we get a tray of something in here?

That does it. She's crying now, or trying not to. She might even be relieved if I asked for Lee at this point, but I don't want Lee anymore, not in this room with its electric bed that does things and the linoleum floor and the vinyl floorboards or whatever it is they've got down there that's ugly and easy to wash. I don't want to see Joanne and Lee together; I could never pretend I didn't see them both clearly in here.

Lunch isn't for a couple of hours, Joanne says. Her voice is subdued. She thinks speaking in a normal voice will provoke me. She says, Would you like me to ask if you can have a snack?

I feel my mouth tightening, chastised in spite of myself. I'll wait, I say.

There's no TV that I can see, nor any radio. They could have brought my kitchen radio, if they'd thought for just two seconds, but then it's always on when I'm at home and maybe this is just their way of voting. Joanne is sitting again in the chair in the corner and I find that I have nothing to say to her, so I close my eyes again and play possum. Even with my eyes closed, though, I can't stop seeing that pattern of dimples on the drop ceiling above me, and that leaves me wondering if they'll decide that I'm done living alone and sell my house and ask me which few of my possessions I'd like them to move into the assisted-living facility they found and that if I don't like the look of the drop ceiling there either maybe I could look out my new window at the nice landscaping on the other side of the parking lot, instead.

I wonder if they'll even tell me if I'm dying, that I'm finally pegging out and that look Joanne is wearing is her thinking of everything she'll have to do once I'm gone, of her own life that will stop for a time while I become accustomed to being in the ground.

I don't think anyone will tell me outright if they expect me to live or die. Folks aren't brave that way anymore, but then maybe most of them never were. I suppose I'll know there's hope if they give me stern looks and instructions to pour out my bourbon and get more roughage, to eat oatmeal or tree bark or some such thing, and then of course I'll know there's not if they come at me with kindly smiles and ask if my pillows are all right, because they none of them expect me to leave this place.

My heart is beating. I didn't die, I know that much for sure. I'm stuck here in this room with my head clear and far too much to think about. I know Joanne will be here the entire time, whether I want her here or not. Lee is somewhere in this hospital, but not in this room because she's afraid of seeing me or having to be with Joanne or both. I want them to cremate me, but that I'll have to write down because they'll neither of them tolerate my saying it out loud. I know far better than either Joanne or Lee realize what it is they're feeling right now, because I've seen my own mother and father into the ground, and because I was the one left to stick the pieces of our lives together when Garfield up and died.

I know that Joanne and Lee will be powerless to control the thoughts appearing on their faces when they're looking down on me in this bed. I know that I've missed my own sister Estelle more than I would have guessed, and that I've missed Porter, my brother, even more than I feared I would. I know that once I'm gone there will be no one left who can point at a picture of my mother and her twin and say for certain which girl is which. That there is no one left at all who knew me when I was Maggie Doud. That only Porter and Estelle understood why, when I became a wife, I said my name as if it were a private joke, because no matter how long I lived or how many years I wore Garfield's ring I would never truly think of myself as Margaret Maguire. That I begrudged, if only slightly, Porter's ability to remain a Doud and even give that name to others. I know that I reproach myself each time I pass Garfield in the living room, sitting there in his Army uniform in his frame on his shelf, and that he's sitting there still for the very reasons I held my tongue when both Joanne and Lee divorced.

I know that the pain I felt last night, pacing the house in my nightgown, that pain like a vise that left me breathless and sweating cold is gone now, and I know what I was thinking as I walked and walked the floors, afraid of sitting even as I weakened, afraid of what might happen if I stopped just once. I know I felt Garfield there, felt that he was there somewhere, and that I was looking for him. I walked through each room without turning on a light because after forty years I know the corners of my furniture as well as anyone can know anything, and because the dark carries different things than the light, like sheet music forgotten on the piano by a child, and the aroma of cigars, and the certain feeling that a man's—a husband's—coat and hat are hanging behind the closet door.

The wind was in the chimney and I knew that it was getting colder out, the way the heat kept cycling on. I pulled open the curtains on the picture window to look out and saw that it had started to snow. I could see the streetlight near the bridge through the black branches of my trees and the snow caught in a ferocious swirl in its cone of light. The arms of the magnolia and the pear tree were still swept clean, but drifts were beginning to grow against the yew hedge that divides my property from the next. The wind kept up its crying to get past my flue, and the sound pressed in on me so that I went to the front door and unlocked the deadbolt and then stood there a moment trying to remember the last time I had unlocked that door, because it was the kitchen door we had always gone in and out of. And then I opened the closet door by the piano and went through it past the coats there and through the door on its other side to Garfield's old office.

I could see plainly that it was the guest room I was standing in, that I'd made into a bedroom for Lee after Garfield died. I knew that the bed beneath the windows, the dresser, and the nightstand had all stood there for decades, but they still surprised me and I put my hand on the cold edge of Garfield's little sink on the wall to reassure myself, leaned against it, and looked at the floor, remembering the mark Garfield's dentist's chair had left on the linoleum, the ring so badly worn into the tiles that I'd had to put down carpeting to cover it after they took the chair away.

What had I been thinking, making Lee sleep in here all those years, with just that door between her and the old waiting room and not even the flimsiest lock on it to reassure her that she was truly closed off from the room where her father had died? I'd slept in here, myself, when Joanne and Stephen had still been married and I'd put them in the big bedroom when they visited. I suppose I thought I was exorcizing ghosts by making everyone pretend it was an ordinary room, that the ring mark on the floor and the sink on the wall were things you might find in any bedroom. But last night I wanted to get the hammer and nails right then and seal it all off. I didn't need anything in either of those rooms. Not the bed, the dresser, the nightstand, the radio or the lamp, nor the lawn chairs and suitcases and Christmas ornaments in the next room, the last room, that I only ever went into when I had to because I couldn't be in there longer than it took to get something or put it back.

I knew better, standing there in my nightgown, but I opened that last door. To scare myself, I suppose. To see whether Garfield was in there, with his hand on the knob on the opposite side, turning it with me, letting me in because he'd had enough of waiting and had finally come to get me. But it was a storeroom, just a storeroom, and it had been for nearly forty years. I'd never taken down the old venetian blinds in that room or any other, though these were always left open now. The walnut coat tree for patients still stood on the right side of the door. The chairs for waiting in and the little round table were there in back against the wall underneath the boxes they held up for me now. Even the key to the drop-front desk still stood in the lock in the drawer like a child's stuck-out tongue.

There was no Garfield, of course, nor any chalk outline or pool of blood because there never had been chalk or blood, just a man in his late forties, balding slightly and running to fat, neatly and inconveniently dead on the floor. Still, I began to shake with panic, standing there in that cold room. My breath came shorter and shorter and I felt more tired than I can remember ever being. I wanted to get back out of there, to slam the door shut because of the feeling that my girls were standing right behind me, because the sound of my own screaming was coming back to me and with it the image of Garfield, there on the floor where I'd found him. I felt as if I were going to be sick, but I made my way back out of that room and into the hall and somehow dialed my neighbor Evelyn's number. I couldn't hear with the blood thundering in my ears, and the dark was suddenly too dark to see anything, but I clamped my hand to that receiver and said Evelyn! again and again, as loudly as I could, until everything was black and quiet and I couldn't say it anymore.

That's just what Garfield did, called a name without anyone's answering. Called and called it until he had to lie down on the floor knowing he would never get up again. Everything was over, everything was done, and when we found him I saw the girls' faces that were both stricken and relieved and I wondered if they would ever be able to say that it was good that he was gone. I imagined a picture of the three of us then, as real as any snapshot, just me and the girls who were suddenly only mine, and we were smiling, even though I knew that in that instant of terror and in spite of the relief there wasn't anything any one of us wouldn't have given to get him back again. There was only Garfield's gleaming head on the linoleum, and me, flooded with pity and scorn and rage because he was nothing more than an insignificant corpse on an insignificant floor.

And now I'm crying in this bed in this sun-filled room because of Garfield alone in that room, because of me alone last night in the hall with the phone still in my hand, because I want to go home, because Lee is here beside the bed now, asking me if I can open my eyes, asking me what's wrong. I'm crying because Joanne and Lee will be circling me now, and circling each other to work out everything they need to know before I die. And I'm crying because they still haven't realized that I've been circling myself all these years, trying and failing to be brave, trying to riddle out the truth of it and portion out the blame in all the places it should lie.

— 3 —

They named me Margaret Susannah Doud. Susannah, for my mother's own mother, who was German-born, and Margaret because it was the only name both my father and mother could agree on. It had belonged to no one on either side of the family, Dad had reasoned, so no feelings could be hurt in using it. Most of all, he said, he simply loved the sound of it. He never reconciled himself to hearing people call me Maggie, though, and would make as if he were puzzled when my school friends came to the door asking if I could come out to play.

Maggie? he'd say, sometimes stretching the act to squinting into the distance and scratching his head. Maggie . . . Oh, you want Margaret!

He'd smile, though, even when Mother called me every nickname she could think of to get his goat. She'd call me to dry the dinner dishes, singing, Maggie Peggy Magpie! and he'd tease back and call her Ada, which made Mother stamp her foot and scowl, on the off chance he meant it and had confused her with her twin. He'd grab her then and kiss her and whisper *Emma Emma Emma* in her ear, and she'd swat at us kids with whatever was to hand to make us leave the room if we hadn't already gone.

I was the baby, and Porter, who was older by four years, called me Dolly. Estelle was in the middle, two years behind Porter and two ahead of me. She called me Sappo. Dad would sigh at this behind his newspaper and say, Why on earth did we trouble ourselves to name her Margaret? And Mother, who'd had it from a Swedish neighbor, would say, A much-loved child has many names, and Dad would lower his paper and say, Is that a fact, as if it truly were the most interesting thing he'd heard that day.

My childhood was unpunctuated by grief. My greatest sorrow, as a girl, was that Estelle was beautiful. More than her fair share, it seemed to me, as if she'd filched bits from the rest of us. If I'd known the word changeling as a child, I'd have hurled it at her to make her sorry, but it would have done no good. Estelle was a pain, but she wasn't superior or mean; she truly had no idea how it bruised a person to stand next to her and know that the air stopped glowing when it got to you.

A string of boys broke our doorbell twice, trying to get at her, and Dad finally dismounted it and made them knock instead. I puzzled at the peculiar expressions that overtook Mother and Dad's smiles when they'd waved Estelle off on another of her dates. They looked sad, as if they were both just back from the future and it didn't look good. I knew they trusted Estelle and, though she looked as if she were made of gauze, we all knew she could throw a punch because Porter had taught her himself. They had that same sad look again when Estelle showed up ready-married to Jack, as if they somehow already knew he was only husband number one, and I realized they were worried it was her profile he had married, or the tick-tock swing of her rear.

Porter was a gangly child, all arms and legs that seemed to sprout directly from his neck. He grew to be a rangy man like Dad, and he had Dad's eyes. We knew Porter's ears came straight from Mother, but she helped us all to imagine they were his own outlandish invention by keeping hers out of sight, under hair she arranged and pinned in swoops that showed only her lobes.

Porter was kind. There's no other word for it. I could also say that he was gentle and patient and good, but all of those things came from his kindness. When I started losing baby teeth and he called me a Toothless Gooseberry Hopper, I never took offense because there was no meanness when he said it. He just smiled and you felt that you always knew what he was thinking, because there was nothing he needed to hide. He was never teased or bullied that I knew of in school; the boys all understood that, even if they goaded him, even if one of them asked to stand under one of Porter's ears on a rainy day, he would simply have obliged and leaned over, pulling outward on the tip of his ear. It was too much work to rile such a contented person.

He was outside more than he was in. He would have slept outside if he could have convinced Mother to let him. I always thought that was why he chose the railroad, and not because he wanted to be like Dad. If Porter was a conductor, too, it was because trains moved through a varied landscape. You might be inside a train car, but you had only to look outside to see rivers, fields, hills, and cities. I always wondered how he reconciled himself to the speed of trains, though, because as a boy, he liked nothing better than to sit quite still, outside.

Porter took me to see the frogs. Estelle didn't want to come. She preferred to stay clean at home and balance her doll, sitting up, across from her on the bedroom rug for a tea party. At the pond with Porter, I knew somehow without his telling me to sit quiet and wait. Just sit on the bank as he did, with my chin on my knees, and watch the water. The frogs were right there in plain sight, of course, but it took a while to see them, even when you'd had some practice. I thought at first that I'd only see them if they splashed the water's surface to gulp at bugs, but then I saw one near a small patch of lilies, just as still as I was, watching me. I saw its oily head, and then its body, sloping away under the water, and then, suddenly, there were endless pairs of humped bronze eyes looking at me from just above the water, and I laughed.

Porter had seen them already, and had been watching me. I don't believe either of us said a word, but I remember feeling a deep contentment at the look I saw on his face. He'd known that I would see the frogs without his pointing, and he was pleased to have been the one to show me. I remember a cushion of mosses under my palms, and a pink toadstool growing under a tree. Acrid pine oil on my fingers from a branch I used to lift a frantic moth from the water. These other things come to me in flashes, though, like photographs held up and snatched away.

Porter's smile was a benediction, and never more so than after he and Frances had lost their Barbara Jean and he came to the hospital to see Joanne in my arms and smiled as if he'd never once known sorrow. It seemed that his experience of joy was deeper, amplified by wisdom and loss. His smile that day was the same smile I had seen at the frog pond, and I saw it again after Lee was born, and then again, when Joanne became a mother, and he first saw Melissa.

And when Melissa was just four or so, and Porter was an old man, all outsized ears and nose, with a flat-top they must have trimmed against a level, she looked up at us from his recliner and announced that the next time she visited him and Frances she was going to sleep there all night with the leg rest up, it was that comfortable. We beamed at her, Porter, Frances, and I, and I thought, you savor this you precious girl. This is how I looked at six or seven, when I was the girl smiling at Porter. When I had just seen the frogs.

It happens all the time, if you remember to see it, if you remember to realize that it's happening. No one ever need say the words. A man declares himself with a naked gaze. A child stares, truly sees you, and is content. A brother watches you see-ing something for the first time.

I go back to the beginning, or as near to it as I can come, hop-ing that I'll see the warning, the place I first got it wrong. How did Porter find Frances, and Estelle finally find Harry? How did Mother find Dad, and how did I, who was loved, have a choice and still get it wrong?

I believe now that Porter took me to the frog pond to let me know that I could understand anything worth understanding by being watchful and patient and by waiting until the thing showed itself to me. You might say that he couldn't have known that, that he was only a child himself, but he likely thought it a plain enough fact that the truths in our lives are all right there to be seen if we let ourselves see them, which makes my only real tragedy the fact that I never looked longer at myself.

$\mathcal{T}$hey won't let you sleep in this place. I'd like to know
how they think a person is meant to get better if every
time you close your eyes the door flies open and someone with a
needle or a paper cup of pills comes blowing in and snapping on
the light. And when they leave again, they do it just as fast and the
lights go out and the door falls shut behind them with a whoosh
that you feel all the way over in your bed.

It's boring, of course, during the day, and if you've got a book
you wish it were a different book, and if you're lonely, you want
company until the company is sitting there looking stricken and
you wish they'd just go away because it's not you that's supposed
to be doing the comforting, and wouldn't they please go out in
the hall and find out what the doctor thinks and when you can
go home, because all you really want is to be bored and lonely
there, instead.

I have to take the IV stand with me for a trip to the toilet, and
it obeys me like an old dog. One of the nurses is waiting in the
room when I come out and she knows better than to come and
help me over to the bed.

I thought maybe you'd escaped, she says. She's smiling, but I
can see she's also waiting for me to hurry it up.

As if I'd be seen anywhere outside this room looking like
this, I say.

Would you like a sponge bath today?

Would I like a bath? I try to sound injured, but she's smiling at me the way Melissa does, and I'm in no mood to sass someone who thinks it's charming. She undoes my gown a little before I get into the bed and pulls it down and off my arms once I'm sitting. She's wringing out her cloth when Lee walks in.

Give us a minute! I say, but she's coming across to the bed anyway.

Turn around, I tell her. Give me some privacy.

Mom—

I'm entitled to what privacy I can have while I can still have it, I say. Now, turn around.

The nurse is just giving me a vigorous rub above the waist, and she's done so quickly I raise my finger to stop her when she goes to pull my gown back up. The tiniest smile flutters across her face, and then she fusses some with my sheet and blanket, snapping and fluffing, making noise, taking her time.

I ask Lee, Where's Joanne gotten to?

Buying coffee. You were out at home.

Where are you two sleeping? I wink at the nurse and flap a hand at her. You can turn around now, I tell Lee.

In our old rooms. Why?

The door is falling shut again behind the nurse, and Lee is dragging the room's only chair over by its arms. If Joanne's in her old room, that means she didn't need my double bed because Bill hasn't come with her, and that means I'm not dying.

I want to go home.

I'll bet you do, but they haven't said anything about that yet.

Ask them.

I think they still need to monitor you a while longer.

It's more pronounced, I'm noticing, her sounding like the parent. It's been coming for a while and she'll be feeling more

entitled, become more entrenched, now that I've had this epi-
sode. It's funny that Joanne is the one who hesitates to boss me,
but then she's always been so easily cowed. Lee would give me
such a look of scorn if I told her that I think she's the bossy one.
Depending on her mood, she'd either snort and holler *Could've
fooled me*, or sit there and shake her head and cry. If I thought Lee
would hear me, I'd tell her that she'd never thought it through,
that she'd never paid attention and seen that Joanne could be
undone by shame. I knew that Joanne had bossed Lee past endur-
ance since the day she was born; I'd been there for it all. But I also
knew why she did it and where she'd learned the bully's trick of
striking hard and striking first.

Mom, she says. What is it?

She's leaning forward in that chair now, and if she gets out of
it I'll never be able to control my voice.

I don't want to be here anymore. I want to go home.

Well, all right, I'll ask, but I don't see what the hurry is.

Christmas.

Christmas? she says, as if I've uttered something truly improb-
able, and I'd like to tell her that she sounds just like Joanne. She's
right in a way, of course. I don't lift a finger at Christmas anymore. They come to me and do everything. I preside and admire
the tree and tell them where to find the crystal salt and pepper shakers when it's time to set the table because I move them
secretly every few years to keep them off balance and to keep
myself necessary.

I know that Joanne will be the one to worry about Christmas,
that she'll contrive to be the one who decides the menu, even
though she knows very well that the rest of us just want the things
we want and nothing more. She can make stuffing just like my
mother's, but that's not interesting enough for her, and she knows
good and well that I only ever made my scalloped oysters for Gar-

field and that no one else can abide them, but she still makes them just the same, as if Garfield is expected, back from the dead, and is bringing Elijah with him to dinner. And she knows we like the canned cranberry sauce precisely because we're used to it and we don't need any of her sauce from scratch. Why would I want uncooked cranberries at all? I don't care how long she's chopped them or how much sugar she's dumped on them or how glossy the page in the magazine was when she checked to see how much fresh orange juice was supposed to go in. I like putting my mother's crystal cranberry dish out on the table because Mother was proud of that silly thing, proud that she owned a dish we needed just twice a year to put a log of jelly on. And I like hearing that same laughter when everyone finally notices that I've put the unopened can of cranberry sauce on its side on the dish again and someone gets me the opener so we can all hear the suck of air when the jelly lets go of the can and plops out onto the dish and then all watch it squirm when the first person cuts it.

I know Joanne will keep Melissa busy at the stove all day while she directs traffic with a tinkling glass of scotch in one hand. She'll call the meal *her gift* to us all, which will be true enough in the planning and paying for it, if less so in the actual execution. Oh, she won't want Lee to lift a finger with the food; no, no, she's got it all worked out. Couldn't Lee iron the napkins, instead? Couldn't Lee just go sit down? She'll send Bill in to circle the room with the bottle of scotch and then with the wine while we wait for dinner, keeping us greased up and easy, making it less startlingly obvious that the only person Joanne trusts to get things right is Joanne. And by the end of the meal, she'll sit there silent and looking bruised, taking stock of what was left uneaten on the table, the dishes we didn't appreciate.

If I told Joanne to leave Melissa be and let her keep me company, she'd only remind me of all the holidays I tied her into one of my aprons and left her at the stove, and she'd be right. But it infuriates me all the more because she's older than I was then and she should know by now that it's the people sitting at your table that you'll remember, not the food. The food doesn't matter. The candlelight matters, and the light from the tree because you'll always remember the quality of that light on your favorite faces. The way the shadows fell and you couldn't quite make out Porter's eyes at the other end of the table, but you knew from experience that he was smiling at Frances with them while she talked. Or maybe he was looking at Melissa, still little, full of dinner and fighting sleep, watching the candles and the crystal twinkling. And then the faces of the husbands who died or got sent packing creep in on you, and you try not to see them, because they were such a sad waste of time and you knew it then. Or maybe it was just a waste, and there's one you miss. And once you've let the others' husbands in, you think of your own and the way he always seemed to take up two places at the table and use up all the air in the room. Then you've gone so far back you have to stare down at the streaks of gravy and cranberry sauce on your plate and hope that no one asks you what you're thinking.

It all goes slippery then, and you're at your mother's table, not your own. You're young enough that no one expects you to help much, and the dinner is a magic trick your mother performs. You stare at her across the table because she's not young anymore, but she's not old yet, either, and you remember her like this. The skin on her arms and under her chin is just starting to go loose. She isn't pretty. You wonder if she ever was, but then you know it doesn't matter because your father is looking at her as if she is. She's wearing the earrings you keep in your jewelry box now but never wear, yourself. They wink in the candlelight when she turns her head; you try to remember who gave them to her. And now it's your mother who is remembering and staring at her plate in a sad, fond sort of way, and she's slipping away from you. The room is going dark at the edges and your mother is receding, and then someone is clattering the plates and asking if there's anything more you want, and you're an old woman again in your own living room sitting at a folding table covered with your wedding linen, and the ghosts have left the table.

·—5—·

 hen Estelle's first husband Jack was killed it had been no one's fault but the Germans', and we all found that the helplessness of it made it easier to comfort Estelle. Easier, anyhow, than having to watch him waste away with illness, easier even than if he'd been struck and killed by an automobile. It wasn't fated, exactly, but we all knew the odds were that Garfield would come home from the war and Jack would not. Because he was a dentist, the Army gave Garfield an oak leaf to go with his caduceus, and sent him to a base in the Pacific, but Jack, because he was a tradesman who'd never even finished high school, was given boots and a gun and landed on the ground in France.

There wasn't much anyone could say, then, when Estelle turned up with the telegram in her hand, and we all coped by going through her finances with her and deciding for certain that she could keep the little house she and Jack had bought if she got back her job at the telephone company. Porter even figured that she'd have a little extra, and she bought herself a standard poodle and named him Jacque.

But sitting with Estelle, the two of us staring at Jack's name on that yellow paper, did not prepare me in any way for finding her again at my kitchen table, just a handful of years later, bewildered and sobbing because she was divorcing Walter. She pulled the rug out from under me, and then Lee and Joanne did too, by turns.

21

Married for years, then suddenly not. Lee was just as bewildered as Estelle had been, and through her sobbing I remembered Porter helping Estelle, and simply told her I wanted to see her checkbook. And when Joanne told me that she and Stephen were divorcing, she never even met my eye. The whole thing was too distasteful, and she delivered the story to the kitchen table instead of to me, all the while wearing a look that suggested I had been the one to pinch up her dirty underthings and strew them around the room.

Sons and a brother given to me, then sent away. Though it was decades on and there was no war involved, Joanne's divorcing Stephen felt like losing Jack. I knew that it had been just as inevitable and just as sorry a waste the same as I knew that Joanne had been careless with him, indifferent to the care she owed him. I found I couldn't meet her eye any more than she could meet mine, and since my role in these conversations was not to offer my opinion, I asked to see her checkbook, too.

I don't know that Estelle would ever have divorced if Jack had lived through the war. And her second husband Walter, poor man, was nothing more than a Band-Aid for her after Jack, and that was certainly the reason he strayed. There was hardly dust on their wedding photo before he was out the door again, and then finally Estelle was as dispassionate as anyone could ever have wished her to be and waited years before she married Harry. By then her jawline and her middle had both gone soft, and though she still always looked as if she'd just come from the hairdresser's, she was finally only pretty, and drifting toward pleasant-looking, like me. Harry had come back from the war without his left hand, and he kept a white glove on the wooden one he wore instead with both his shirtsleeves down and buttoned tight, even in summer. They were both imperfect and too old to have children, and we all breathed out when Estelle found him, because we knew it meant that she was done.

I knew that each and every one of their divorces were because of infidelity, and although I could have told them all that it was poor choice on their parts that had led one way or the other to the infidelities, I didn't. Garfield had never strayed. They knew it and I knew it. It wasn't that he'd never been caught, he simply hadn't strayed, and if he'd given me other reasons to want to divorce him, I've never believed in divorce, and in any case he was dead before I could truly reach the end of my tether.

It was a minor scandal, of course, when Estelle divorced Walter, but it followed close enough upon the war that people were still unnerved and eager to sidestep any new unpleasantness. Everyone, even the folks at church, agreed somehow to overlook Walter, and resurrect Estelle the War Widow in lieu of Estelle the Divorcée. So I'd had some practice by the time Lee and then Joanne each came to me. Practice in holding my tongue when what I wanted was to inventory the facts, to reconstruct for Joanne the moment Stephen had walked into my kitchen and offered a harmless opinion on the wedding lists Joanne had spread out to show me on the table. It was his wedding to her that she was planning, after all; she'd hit a snag, and he offered a solution. But she didn't hear it, she couldn't have heard it, because even before the sound of his voice had died in the room she snapped, This doesn't concern you. If he'd turned on his heel, right then, right there, I'd have shaken his hand and wished him well. He took the blow, though, and before he could go back to whatever it was that was on the television, Joanne was scowling at her papers again, and I thought, there you have it, if you were wondering. There's your marriage, right there.

Lee divorced before Joanne, though, and it was the only time she beat Joanne to the punch and did something that seemed, on the surface at least, to be original. When she sat sputtering and sobbing and asked me to tell Joanne so she wouldn't have to,

I almost laughed. She was finally learning, and if what she was learning was not to trust people, well, so be it. I could only imagine what would come out of Joanne's mouth if I told her Lee had come home to Barry soaping up a blonde in their shower. I left that out, of course, and when Joanne did ask what had happened I looked straight at her and told her it wasn't any of her business. Because all she'd said when Lee first showed her the diamond Barry gave her was, Oh. Because even if she'd been right about Barry, she hadn't smiled in their wedding photos. I hadn't wanted to smile, either, but I'd looked over at Lee while the photographer was lining us all up, knowing she'd be beaming, and that was enough. I had once stood in a wedding dress beside an arrogant man. I had once been unheeding of the troubled faces around me.

Lee slept in her old room the night she left Barry. It hadn't been just the two of us in the house since Joanne had been away at college. I put my box of tissues on her nightstand and left the room's two doors ajar, to the living room and to the kitchen, so she'd have a little light and so she could hear me until I went to bed, as if she were still ten years old and afraid of the dark. I sat on the davenport then and put all of the photos from her wedding in a manila envelope and stuck the envelope in a hatbox on the hall closet shelf. She would have been able to hear me and even guess at what I was doing, and I don't know what I would have said if she'd come out and asked me to stop. Asked her to sit, maybe, and told her she could do what she liked with her own album, but this was what I was doing with mine. Passed her the group photo and asked her to tell me what she saw.

What was plain to me was that Melissa was the only one besides Lee who was truly smiling in that photo, with her flower girl basket and her tiny white gloves. We'd lost Frances by then, and Stephen stood with Porter on the end by Barry's best man, both of them looking pleasant and dignified, both of them wise enough to know that the photo wasn't about them. Joanne looked like she'd just caught a whiff of something smelly and she was put out that she couldn't break her pose long enough to fan it away. Barry smirked, there's no other word for it, as if he were just waiting for the flash so he could kiss Lee's cheek and tell her, Don't wait up, honey; I've got a date. His father, too. The two of them, entitled to anything they could get away with and shrugging, *What's a fellow to do?* I've never known precisely what the look on Barry's mother's face was, but then I also knew I didn't want to look at it long enough to decide. I looked like what I was: a widowed grandmother in a lace dress and hat. Someone who didn't like having her picture taken. Someone who didn't show her teeth when she smiled.

After Lee got shot of Barry, she decided, like me, that enough was enough. No sense in risking a repeat if you can keep a roof over your own head. Joanne, to my great surprise, and I suppose to her credit, didn't give up. Her Bill is a lot like Estelle's Harry was, come to think of it. He's steady and calm; nothing ever happens fast when Bill's involved, but it happens just the same. He doesn't hover, and he doesn't smother you with worrying.

Bill is older than Joanne by ten years, which puts the two of us on a more equal footing. He remembers the time before the war, which allowed for a kind of shorthand between us, and shrank the time we needed to get to know each other at first. He isn't my son, though, not the way I allowed Stephen to be. I can't risk that again, even if I don't believe Bill's going anywhere. All the same, he's family. Someone who can see me in my housecoat and slippers. Someone who can open my refrigerator or turn my television on without asking.

I'm not surprised, then, when the nurse comes with my discharge papers and then Joanne comes in with Bill right behind her. It makes me peevish at first, as if it's Joanne's way of telling me to behave myself, and then I feel more peevish still when I have to admit that she's right. I do generally think about what I say before I say it if Bill's around. Then Joanne gives me a bruised look, of all things, when I say I'll feel better hanging onto Bill between the car and my kitchen door than I would her or Lee. I look right back at her and I'm surprised when I see an overweight woman in middle age whose elderly mother has just had a heart attack. I don't mean to say that I don't recognize her. I still see my daughter standing there, but I'm dismayed to see that she's angry, that what is uppermost in Joanne's mind is the fact that Joanne is being inconvenienced. She's missed work, she's been made to worry, although whether she's worried that I'm dying or that I'm dragging it out, I have no idea. I know I shouldn't let her provoke me, that it's none of her doing if I see both Garfield and his mother Lillian in her expression right now, but I'm past pretending not to be riled and I say, Melissa would have done just as well. She doesn't boss me, either.

The nurses tell me to enjoy Christmas and not to come back until at least next year, and Bill gets me into the car. He holds the rear passenger door open for Joanne, and that makes me smile. He's not going to let her drive while she's in a mood and there's snow on the ground. She'd just show off. Take a corner too fast to show me how she could recover from a slide, whereas Bill knows better than to get into the slide in the first place. You never feel as if you're being driven with Bill. Summer or winter, he gets you from A to B, and you haven't felt a thing. Not a curve, not a bump. It's not much of an exaggeration to say that the wipers seem to work better when he's driving. I wonder what Garfield would have made of Bill.

This makes me want to giggle, and to cover up I start chattering about the houses along Main. If Joanne's hell-bent on being annoyed, I'll oblige and be annoying. Bill just chuckles at me, which makes the silence from the back seat all the more evident.

I say, What on earth is that supposed to be? A stuffed Santa up on the roof? This one here's always dark. I suppose they go someplace warm at Christmas. Oh, now, this one coming up. I don't know how the neighbors stand it. It's just dutchie.

Dutchie? Bill says.

She means tacky, Joanne says from behind me. Garish.

I mean dutchie, I say.

Bill says, We can go for a drive after dinner one evening. See them all lit up.

You can all go. I don't believe I care to, I say.

Not even to see the dutchie one? He looks younger suddenly, teasing me like that. Now Joanne will be mad at him, too, and I can't work out whether he doesn't know or if he truly doesn't care.

Bill turns into my drive and says, I put your outside lights up for you.

He's humble, Bill is. He didn't wait for me to notice them, didn't say there was a surprise. He just told me outright.

Well—I don't know what to say.

I thought you might like to have them up.

You didn't need to trouble yourself.

That's all right.

I half expect Joanne to prompt me to say thank you, but even she can hear what's just passed in our voices, and now Bill has me thinking of Porter and his quiet way of showing affection.

Melissa and Lee are waiting on the kitchen stoop, shivering and hugging themselves.

Hello, sickie, Melissa says.

Hello, yourself. Go back inside, the two of you. You don't need to stand there gawking at me.

They only grin harder, of course, and neither of them

budge, which makes me wonder how it is that Joanne's sister and daughter both always know when I'm fooling, and Joanne herself does not.

Once they've got me inside and Bill's helped me through to the living room, I stop.

Oh, no, I say. Not the tree.

I missed it in the daylight when we were coming up the drive, even though they've got the lights plugged in and the drapes wide open. Bill lets go of me once I'm by the davenport, and Lee kisses my cheek.

Merry Christmas, Mom, she says.

What am I supposed to do with that tree? Who's going to take it down?

You won't have to do a thing, Lee says. One of us will be here as long as you need, and we'll take care of the tree.

Well, where is everybody going to sleep?

Joanne finally speaks. Bill and I are going to the Arrowhead, she says. And Missy and Lee will stay here with you.

I don't want you in any motel on Christmas. You and Bill should have my room.

Mom, I'm not turning you out of your own bed. You just had a heart attack.

I know I did, and I don't want to hear any more about it. It makes no difference to me where I sleep, so long as I'm not on the davenport.

Missy will be on the davenport.

She shouldn't have to sleep in the living room, I say.

Then I'll sleep in the living room, Lee says. And Melissa can have my bed.

Melissa yells from the kitchen, Damma, I don't mind! and I start swallowing hard, to keep myself from crying. I only wanted to decide something, anything at all. They don't want me to worry.

They don't want me to have anything to worry about, which will allow them to worry less, and this is important because I've just arrived at number one on all of their to-do lists. But their wanting it and my knowing how to accomplish such a thing, to simply turn off being even nominally in charge, are not the same.

I look around and it's clear that I'm to blame for the looks on all their faces. I might as well be four years old right now, for all the use I am at controlling myself. There was once a Christmas I hid in the kitchen, the way Melissa is staying out of the way in my kitchen now. Our Christmas tree was bare, not a needle on it, and it was my fault. I'd sweet-talked Dad into buying the tree too early, and the fit Mother had when he brought it into the house was nothing compared to the sulk she treated us to when she saw that by Christmas Eve, just as she'd predicted, the tree was nothing more than decorated tinder in an iron stand. Dad blamed himself for giving into me, and went out in a snowstorm to buy another tree. I swept up every last needle while Mother scowled at me from the davenport. No one else was mad; they were all waiting for Mother to decide she was done with her mood so they could tease me about it. And sitting here now, I'm imagining the belly laugh I'd get if Mother could see my artificial tree.

Did I have heart ornaments? I say. I don't remember any heart ornaments.

No, Mom, Joanne says. I made those.

You made them?

They're cookies. They're sugar cookies.

Well, imagine that, I say, and everyone is looking at the tree with my old lights and ornaments and Joanne's heart cookies, and no one need say you're welcome or even thank you. Joanne sits back, easy in her chair, Melissa steps back into the doorway, and everyone breathes out because Damma has decided she's done with her mood and it can be Christmas again.

arfield did beat all.

I'm sure Porter said that more than once, and even he didn't know the half of it. It was impossible to tell, whenever anyone made a statement about Garfield Maguire, whether they were expressing admiration or a desire to wring his neck. He had a sense of justice and fair play, but mostly where they concerned himself. He told me once that, when he was twelve and the circus had come to town, he and a friend agreed to muck out the elephants' stalls in return for free admittance, but when they came back to claim their tickets, the woman who'd struck the deal with them looked at them straight-faced and said, I've never seen you boys before. Garfield jerked his head at his friend and the two of them went off to see if the wheelbarrows were still full of dung. Once they'd emptied them in front of a refreshment stand, they walked the wheelbarrows back over to the woman and left her to wonder what they'd done with the dung. The way Garfield told the story, he smacked his hands clean on his trouser legs, told the woman, I guess you remember us now, and walked right past her and into the circus, free of charge.

If Garfield had heard someone tell a story of injustice like this that didn't end in retribution, he'd have thought the teller a chump, and he'd have said so to his face. Oh, he'd have laughed plenty first. Gar would have shaken his head and clapped the poor fellow so hard on the back he'd never have known for sure if he was being sympathized with or made an object of fun.

My dad realized long before I did that Garfield was a mass of contradictions held together with pomade and a suit. Gar demanded deference, but was characteristically irreverent and disrespectful himself. He justified it by saying that he was only punching holes in other people's pretensions, but it was always pretension as Garfield saw it, and his distaste was somehow magnified when he perceived it in a member of the military. You might wonder how he fared at all well in the Army if he was always just this side of insubordination and not always out of earshot when he called his superior a chicken colonel, but you had only to remember that he'd once been the boy with the wheelbarrow of elephant dung before it all began to make sense. My father had initially raised an approving eyebrow when he realized that Garfield habitually called me Margaret, but when Gar told him he'd worked on the railroad as a baggage slammer during college, Dad scowled, and then scowled some more after he tried to correct him and Garfield replied, No, sir, I didn't handle any baggage. I slammed it.

Garfield claimed he didn't believe in taking advantage of people weaker than himself, but then he applied this maxim according to whim, as he did everything else. Any normal person would think a man in need of a nighttime extraction was deserving of pity, but Garfield hung a sign on the side of the house that said only *G. Maguire, D.D.S.*, and said that if a person didn't know that that meant he was available around the clock, he certainly wasn't going to tell them.

Garfield's notion of what constituted weakness grew equally thin whenever he felt he needed a laugh. He'd stuff a patient's mouth full of every instrument he had to hand, and then, liberal and conservative by turns, he'd start talking politics or even just ask what the man thought of the centaur on our cupola, knowing very well that, even if he went outside and pointed right at the weathervane atop our garage, a less educated man still wouldn't be able to say which was which. It was only devilry, he said, brooking no suggestion that it was unjust. How could it be, he said, if he applied it equally to the town millionaire and the one-armed paperhanger from the other side of the tracks? Never mind that none of his patients would argue with a man who had a drill going in their mouth. The very last time I asked what he'd been cackling about, he told me he'd asked a patient his opinion of the geraniums in the window boxes outside his office windows. They were fakes—he'd let the real ones die of thirst—but the poor man, with his mouth full of metal or cotton or both had only dared to flatter. Oh, fine, fine, he'd said. Very beautiful, which made Garfield roar. I stopped asking after that.

It's fair to say that Garfield had one set of rules for himself, and another for everyone else, and in this Joanne is his heir. It's rare that you get through a meal with Joanne without her sneering at something or someone. It can be anything: a lack of sophistication (Oh, no! Your strong suit is never ever your forté; it's your *forte*), to the homeless (I give to several excellent charities, and none of them sit on street corners). If there's a thing to be disparaged, she'll find it, and then she'll all but empty the sour cream dish till you can't even see her baked potato anymore, and pick up the T-bone from the steak she's just polished off and keep eating at it like it's an ear of corn and she's at the family picnic. It's hypocrisy, pure and simple, to insist on perfection and then behave poorly yourself, knowing that everyone around you is too well mannered to tell you you're a fraud.

No one ever seems to know more about any subject than Joanne. She learned that trick from Garfield, too. It saves her from ever looking foolish, from the risk of being corrected, however gently. It saves her having to say, *I don't know*, and allows her to expound instead and reveal ignorance where she sees it. What it doesn't do is save anyone's feelings but her own. She'd claim she's as egalitarian as her father, and that correcting misinformation is not only a service, but a duty, and I won't argue insofar as I've seen her do it to absolutely everyone. Just last year, she thought of a joke while we were at a restaurant, and after we'd all chuckled at it, she decided she'd tell it to the busboy while he was clearing our plates. I shook my head and frowned at her, but she couldn't restrain herself, wouldn't restrain herself, and she asked him if he'd heard about the new male strip club opening out on the highway. To his credit, he realized it was the setup for a joke, and he smiled and said, No . . . And then the smile slid right off his face when she said, It's called Hepplewhites, because it was clear that, whatever the joke meant, Joanne had never expected him to understand.

I was fit to be tied and I told her off in a low voice that everyone else pretended not to hear. Joanne laughed and said, Well, now he knows something more about Georgian furniture, and waved for the check. I grabbed Melissa's arm as we were leaving the restaurant and told her, Help me find that boy, and when she did I took a twenty out of my pocketbook, closed his hand around it, and said, That's just for you. You don't share that with the others. I walked out muttering about the likelihood of his spitting in Joanne's food next time and said nothing else the rest of the evening.

It all comes from insecurity, really, and fear, and although I know Joanne's fear of looking foolish comes from her fear of Gar, of his humiliating her, I don't know what it was that Gar was afraid of. I never met his father or knew Gar to speak much of him, so I'm only guessing if I say that it was his mother Lillian who made him afraid through excessive criticism or too-high expectation, but he was just as fearful as Joanne was of looking foolish. It was fine to tell people he'd been to college and dental school besides, and that his mother had been an educator, but the truth was that she'd taught in a one-room schoolhouse in rural Iowa at the turn of the century, and since that did not give him the cosmopolitan sheen he required, he got that himself. Even after he was done at the university, he read constantly, on every subject, long into the night. His bedtime stories for the girls could be about anything. Dan'l Boone and the Grapevine Swing one night, a far-reaching lecture on Ancient Egypt the next. More nights than I can remember, I found him asleep on the sofa with a book, or more often a volume of the *Britannica* open on his chest. One morning not long after he died, I noticed the B volume of his *Britannica* was missing from the shelf, and I knew without looking that I would find it in bed with Joanne.

The day Gar realized that our pronunciation of English was provincial marked a watershed, and I remember feeling glad that Lillian was no longer alive, so I wouldn't have to watch him go about improving her, too. One of his patients was an elderly woman who'd been born back East, and when she asked about the design and construction of our house, she became puzzled when Garfield told her something about the *ruf*. She said, The what? And he said it again, until she laughed and exclaimed, Oh! The roof!

That was that. I don't know how he found out what was right, but suddenly everything we said was wrong, and I was left more often than not feeling like a child scolded into the corner. The day I found Joanne, all of four years old, sitting outside on his office steps practicing saying, I *catch* the ball. She *catches* the ball, when she'd been happy saying ketch only the day before, I stopped talking and wrote Garfield notes. If I'd complained or tried to reason with him, he wouldn't have heard me, or worse, he would have laughed and told me not to be silly. I'd long since had enough of his ignoring me or condescending. I'd learned that he needed an audience, and that I could needle him fast with silence. By the end of the afternoon, when I'd given him a note that said *We'll be having chicken casserole for dinner, unless you'd prefer the rest of the meatloaf from yesterday*, I could see that the air had gone out of him a bit. He tossed my note in the trash with the other notes and said, All right, Margaret. All right.

The thing I resented most was his lack of imagination and his distrust of it in others. He wasn't one for novels; he preferred to read facts. He'd have said his love of music had less to do with its composition than with the years of training he heard in a virtuoso performance on the radio. This explains his bedtime stories, too, which were all just history lessons in one form or another, and which might sometimes stretch to folk tales, but never so far as fairies. He taught his distrust of imagination to Joanne, though, and what is truly unforgivable, he stamped out any imagination she had herself.

Joanne was a little acquainted with a neighbor lady named Tonty Dunne. No one ever seemed to know her real name or exactly how old she was, only that she'd lived in the little cottage on the corner of 16th and Hedge Avenue for longer than anyone else had been alive. She wore her skirts long, all the way down to her shoes, and when she was outside in her garden, she wore a pinafore just as long and a sunbonnet to shade her eyes. She was tiny and stooped, but she kept an uncommonly beautiful garden and tended it herself. If she grew vegetables, I never saw them through the profusion of flowers surrounding her house every year.

Tonty Dunne lived across the alleyway from Lillian's house, and when we were still living there, Joanne would pass her house on her way to and from school each day. Did you see Tonty Dunne?

I'd ask her when she came home, and she'd nod. Did you say hello? and she'd nod again, and ask, Why doesn't she talk, Mom? She only ever smiles at me. Tonty Dunne never talked to anyone, as far as I knew, but that wouldn't be a good enough answer for Joanne. She's very, very old, I said instead, and when a person gets to be that old, she might just be all talked out.

Sometimes Joanne would come home with a few cut flowers in her fist, and I'd send her over now and then with a small plate of cookies. The plates would come back later, empty and clean, but Tonty Dunne never said a word. I didn't have to imagine their exchanges; I'd seen them for myself. Tonty Dunne on one side of her low wire fence and Joanne on the other. A plate or some flowers changing hands, and Tonty Dunne smiling and waving until Joanne was out of sight, before she went back to her roses.

One winter evening when we'd had a fresh snowfall, Joanne squirmed at the table so badly I asked if she needed the toilet. No, it wasn't that, she said. Tonty Dunne had made a path. She'd seen it on her way home and wanted to go out and see it again, even though it was dark.

A path! Garfield said. Well, I'm glad to hear she can still lift a shovel.

No, not like that, Joanne said. It's a path on the grass.

A path on the grass, Gar repeated, as if he expected her to agree that it was preposterous and wonder with him why she'd said it. Why would she do that?

None of us knew why, and we knew even less when Joanne told us it was a curving path that started at the sidewalk and went across the grass to the curb. I was surprised when Gar did not suggest that Tonty Dunne had finally gone dotty, and even more surprised when he said that we should go see this path.

It'll be gone by morning, he said. We're getting more snow tonight.

And then the three of us stood there in the streetlight, on the sidewalk in front of Tonty Dunne's house, looking at the curving path she'd made in the glittering snow. Joanne walked up to it, but stopped while her feet were still on the sidewalk. I didn't ask what she was thinking; it was plain to see. It looked like a path to somewhere, likely even more so in the dark than it had during the day. It wasn't that it was a path through the snow, or even that it was curved that had her mesmerized. It was Tonty Dunne's path; a curved path she'd made for no apparent reason and without explanation before she went back into her house. And now Joanne was certain that it had been made for her, to take her to another place, if she was only brave enough to set out upon it.

A charitable person might say that Garfield couldn't have known what Joanne was thinking, but I'm certain that he did. He saw Joanne deciding that the path was magic, he told her to walk on it, and without turning around first, without giving me a moment to stop her, just a moment so I could crouch down and look with her at the path in the snow and then take her home without disturbing it and always know that we had seen it and that it had been there, she walked to the end and stopped. When Garfield asked, Where did it take you? Joanne whispered, Hedge Avenue.

And when Tonty Dunne died a few years after of one cancer or another, Garfield went to the hospital every evening to visit her. He took bouquets made with cuttings from her own garden, and told me that it was done with her blessing. He surrounded her with her own flowers, he sat with her and read aloud from the newspaper, and when I asked him why he was lavishing so much time on a woman he hardly knew, he said, Because there's no one else to do it. Garfield was a confounding man. He'd make you see red nine times in a row, and on the tenth he'd do something noble and decent and kind and leave you feeling shamed for thinking ill of him the other nine.

It would be fair to ask what it was I first saw in a man like Garfield Maguire. But I was green. I'd never met anyone like him—there never was anyone like him—and I understood that he was a tyrant only by degrees. I met him by chance, at an afternoon party given by a mutual friend. I saw him across the room and it was clear he'd seen me first and had been looking for a while. He'd been the boy with the wheelbarrow, you see. I never stood a chance.

They were going to give me a tray in bed, but I want my Christmas dinner at the table, the same as the rest of them. There are only five of us, so there was just the one card table to set up. They've got a dark cloth on it I haven't seen before. I say they, but I know it's Joanne. She's gotten out the Spode and found my linen napkins somewhere. I would have used paper, but I suppose since she didn't ask me to do the ironing I can't fuss.

I see that she's been careful and done most things the way I would have done them. She's got red tapers in the candlesticks and not white, and she's left the poinsettia in its green foil wrapper and put it out on a saucer, rather than find a pot. But she's polished and scrubbed everything, or made Melissa do it, and the pepper looks a good deal darker than it used to, which means she's emptied the shaker and refilled it with fresh. I can see that the salt is fresh, too, because there isn't any rice in with it. That one irks me. She'll tell me the rice looks bad and that if I'd just store the shakers empty after the holidays I'd never need it in the first place, and if she does I'll ask her why she of all people doesn't know that the food should land on the table properly seasoned and that the crystal shakers are for show. Just silly twinkly things you get out twice a year to enjoy in the candlelight. I can't say any such thing, though, and I can't use either shaker because then she'll want to hear how it tastes and I'll have to admit that the old salt and pepper were both likely twenty years old.

There aren't any cloves stuck in the ham, and she'll be the only one to have any of those scalloped oysters, but I'll be damned if she hasn't set out a log of cranberry jelly on my mother's crystal dish. We're all holding hands and Lee starts us off on Bless us, Oh Lord, and these thy gifts, and I can't do more than whisper suddenly because I've just seen the dish of my mother's German green beans and I'm trying hard not to cry. They all pretend not to notice, and when I can, I look up and smile and I give Joanne a little nod and Bill passes the beans to me first.

I've put entirely too much food on my plate. It chagrins me how greedy I am, but I'll eat slowly and see how far I get. They're all so quiet. Far too quiet. The food is good, but not so good that they couldn't stop eating for just a moment to compliment Joanne. They're none of them looking at me now, either. They stopped as soon as the last dish was passed and set back on the table, and I realize they're all quiet because they're paying attention. They don't want to miss a single moment because they think I won't be here next year and they'll all be quiet again like this, but they'll be around Joanne's table with no place set for me. I'll grant there's sense in being mindful, but there's no sense at all in grieving me before I'm gone. Estelle did that once with a kitten Dad gave her. It turned out to be sickly, and when Mother told her gently that it likely wouldn't live, Estelle took to her bed and I found her there sobbing and the kitten sitting on the rug watching her, so I put the kitten on the bed and told Estelle she wouldn't be able to play with it when it was dead, so she shouldn't cry over it while it was alive. Estelle looked at me as if she'd never seen me before and, to her credit, dried her face and found a ribbon for the kitten to swat at.

Of course it might not be me they're thinking of. They might truly have gotten lost in thinking about Estelle or Garfield or anyone else who used to sit at this table but is no longer here. I've always wondered at the way people become so melancholy when they sit down to a table with a poinsettia on it. It's dispropor-tionate and unseemly. I can miss Mother and Dad just as well on any old Sunday when I pass their pew in church. And wouldn't they be surprised to see me now at eighty-two. None of them, not one of them, even made it to seventy, and Garfield couldn't even manage fifty. If Estelle were here, she'd look me over and tell me to find my lipstick, but then I'd tell her to take it and draw a smiley face on her rear. Oh, Sappo, she'd say, and flap a hand at me. This one makes me laugh and I sputter a cranberry stain into my napkin. They all look up and want to know what's funny, and I can't have them picturing Estelle drawing red on her saggy behind, so I say instead, Well, Uncle Alf thought it was a hoot.

Thought what was?

The coal he put in our stockings.

You got coal in your stocking?

Melissa's got both eyebrows raised at me, so I guess she's never heard this one, and that makes me wonder how many others I still have to tell her and how much time I have left to do it.

Uncle Alf was Dad's youngest brother, I tell her. He stayed with us one Christmas and got up first so he could take the pres-ents out of our stockings and leave us each with a lump of coal. I thought that was mean. Dad made him give us our presents and say sorry, but Uncle Alf was still smiling when he said it and you could tell he wondered where the harm had been.

I'm frowning now, and I realize they're confused by my hav-ing laughed before I told that story. It's the problem Christmases that stand out, I could say, but that would likely leave Joanne cry-ing into her dinner, so I keep quiet. I see Joanne reaching for her wineglass. She's about to make her annual toast and require us all to drink to *our absent dear ones*, which means Garfield and no one else, so I say, You remember the books, of course, and that stops her so fast I'm surprised she's able to set her glass down again and doesn't just let go of it midair.

Before she can tell it herself, I start, because the first words out of her mouth will be that that was the best Christmas—that there never was a better—when Melissa is sitting right here with us, and for my money the Christmas I was handed my only grand-daughter to hold, a mewling, kicking newborn in a red velvet dress, right here in this room, was better than any stack of books under any tree.

My mother-in-law gave Joanne's father a list of books to order, I say. I address myself to Bill, though I can hardly believe that Joanne would never have told him this story herself. I have no idea what made her think he'd be able to get every one of them so soon after the war, I say, but he wrote away to New York, and he got a stack of books back. Joanne was only six years old that Christmas, but Lillian had taught her to read, and Joanne read every one of those books by herself.

Garfield hadn't even made Joanne wait until morning. Once he'd put the books in a pile right at the front of the tree he went outside and stomped around in the snow and did some deep-throated ho-ho-ho-ing. He even borrowed too-big boots from a neighbor to make footprints he could show Joanne the next morning, step into with his regular shoes on and say, See? Once he'd snuck back inside, he opened and closed the flue a couple of times and rattled around in the grate with the poker, and then waited a little while before he let Joanne come out of her room. They'd been right of course, Lillian and Gar. Joanne ran in bare-foot in her nightgown, and knelt there for the longest time, look-ing through those books.

None of them were wrapped, Joanne says. They were all just there in a stack, so I'd see all of them at once. They were each inscribed *From Santa to a good little girl.*

We had to tell you to read the inscriptions, I say. You were already too busy reading the stories.

And then she says it: Those books saved my life, but Melissa says in the same moment, I read all of them, too, and makes us laugh.

They were all good books, I say, and I'm sorry I started in on the books at all. I'm so tired of hearing how they saved Joanne, how she was trapped in her own mind and no one understood her, which is just another way of saying she was smarter than everyone else around her, and that's her way of saying she was smarter than me. Well, she is smarter than I am, but she wasn't smarter than Gar, and if she thinks I didn't understand her, that I couldn't understand her, she's wrong. I understand Joanne fine, just not in ways she's ever thought of or would like.

You were with us that Christmas, I say to Lee, and Joanne scowls at me for scuppering her memory of the last Christmas she was an only child. I didn't know it yet, I say, but I was pregnant with you.

I smile. Not even Garfield could have gotten us back on track after that one.

$$—8—$$

J could say that Lillian and Gar were too formidable for me. I could claim that I didn't stand a chance, packed off as I was, straight to Lillian's house after the wedding breakfast, that even during the war when Garfield was gone, Lillian was there every day as his proxy. I could even say that I lived those first seven years more as a guest in her house than as family, but that would be making it sound as if I'd felt more welcome than I often did. I've wondered since if the sudden prospect of navigating the remainder of my life as a wife and mother was simply too much for me, and whether I wasn't happier deferring to the two of them. I'd never seen Mother and Dad do anything close to arguing. They teased, they feigned indignation, and then mended things with smiles. I had known Gar and Lillian for years before we finally married, but living with them was thornier than simply knowing them. They were both abundantly set in their ways.

The Depression made it impossible for us to get married, Gar had said, and impossible for him to buy me an engagement ring, what with saving up to start his practice. I had my job at the electric company though, and since Mother and Dad refused to take any money from me for my keep, I set aside quite a lot every month. I got tired of people asking if I'd settled on Gar or if I hadn't—Porter had married Frances, after all, and Estelle was married to her first husband Jack—and finally I went out one day and bought the ring myself. It was admired all around, and no more so than by Lillian, who stretched my hand out across her palm and turned it this way and that to see the fire. She gushed in an outlandish fashion at Gar's extravagance and taste. I glanced at Gar to see if he would correct her misapprehension, and when he avoided my eyes and kept smiling at the ring, I held my tongue.

I knew better than to say it, but I always thought that the war suited Lillian just fine. Garfield was a major in the Army Dental Corps and in no immediate danger, and as long as he was away, I was expected to live in Lillian's house with Joanne. I wondered aloud whether we shouldn't go to Estelle in Cedar Falls for the duration, since Estelle might be glad of the company, what with Jack shipping off to Europe, but they countered that we were already there at Lillian's and that, being younger, Estelle would have less need of me and my pair of extra hands. And then I was reminded of Lillian gloating over Joanne as a newborn, that she was the image of Garfield as a baby and crooning in a nearly exultant singsong, Yes, you'll live with your old Gran, won't you? And your father will go to work, and we'll keep your mother in the basement for milk, and you'll live with me forever. I remembered it, but again I said nothing.

They understood each other, Lillian and Garfield, and operated as one person, never needing to confer or to rehearse a thing. When Garfield was away during the war, I learned that Lillian had his way—or he had hers; it hardly mattered—of announcing a thing by seeming to ask a question about it first. That a decision had already been made became clear by degrees, once you were trapped in the conversation. You could talk all you wanted, you could even argue, but you'd be met with the same barely disguised exasperation until you saw sense, until you finally agreed.

I might have seen it earlier if they hadn't been Catholics, if the decision to raise Joanne as a Catholic hadn't been taken out of everyone's hands by the priest. I agreed to it the day the priest told me it was a condition of marrying Garfield, that they couldn't marry us in a Catholic ceremony—that Garfield couldn't marry me at all—unless I promised. I never minded that, I swear I never did, not until years later when Garfield told me he'd thought it over and decided that I should take Lee to my church, that it wasn't fair that he should have both girls with him at St. Paul's and I should have neither.

What the Pope doesn't know won't hurt him, he said. He grinned when he saw that he'd dumbfounded me, likely thinking I was amazed at his audacity, his liberal thinking, when I was only aghast at the convoluted trick he'd played on me and the priest: toeing the line when it suited him, revealing himself when it had not.

But she's been baptized! I managed to say that much, though I hadn't a clue if I intended to defend or to attack the idea in saying it.

He smiled again, his face untroubled by any awareness of duplicity. Oh, now, he said. I shouldn't think that Presbyterians would let themselves be bothered by a little thing like that.

It troubled me less to be handled this way than they might have thought. If half of Joanne's relatives were Roman Catholics, why shouldn't she be a Catholic, herself? And if her only surviving grandmother had formerly been a schoolteacher, why indeed shouldn't she be the one to teach Joanne to read? It was never the things themselves that were being decided that upset me, it was the elaborate, painstaking way Lillian and Garfield both had of letting me know that managing things and managing me were more trouble than they felt they deserved.

I took to sitting outside, on the porch or the back steps, to let Lillian have the house to herself when I could. Even though it was just the two of us there with Joanne, even with Gar gone, the house felt crowded during the war, and never more so than in the stultifying heat of an Iowa summer.

Lillian took to sitting outside then, when it was hot enough, and I found her already there in her rocker one night after I'd wiped our supper dishes dry and managed to get Joanne to sleep, sticky and flushed on top of her covers. I sat in the straight-backed chair near the screen door. Lillian's rocker creaked the porch boards. She snapped her butter-colored fan, beating time.

She said, Kitchen get too much for you?

I'd swear even the sink light was trying to fry me.

Get yourself a fan, Margaret. This air certainly isn't going to move itself.

I can hardly stand to move, let alone fan myself, I said. I pressed my handkerchief to my forehead and upper lip, and refolded it to wipe the nape of my neck. Gad, I said, I could wring this out.

Lightning bugs pulsed here and there above the grass, cicadas whirred in the trees and hedges. I was watching a gang of gnats spin furiously around the streetlamp at the end of the front walk when Lillian cleared her throat.

Margaret, do I have your permission to teach Joanne to read?

I beg your pardon?

I want to teach Joanne to read. She's not too young, if that's what you're thinking. I taught Garfield and his sisters to read when they were four, but I believe Joanne is bright enough to be taught earlier.

I expect she is, but she'll still be bright in a year or so, I said, frowning a little in surprise, and wondering what I had done to make Lillian's face begin to go so rigid with exasperation.

I've had a letter from Garfield and he approves, she finally said. She took a letter from her pocket and handed it to me. It's on the second page.

I looked at the letter for a moment before I unfolded it, and read from the top of the second sheet, *marvelous if you would teach Joanne* . . .

It would be marvelous if you would teach Joanne to read, Mother, and I heartily approve. That is, I believe, what it says, Margaret.

I breathed out and stopped reading. I refolded the letter and said, It seems to be decided already.

Nonsense, Margaret. Your approval remains.

You and Garfield agree. How can I refuse?

Refuse? Why should you refuse? The ability to read is a great gift to give to a child.

And it is a pleasure to read to a young child, Lillian. I don't believe Joanne wants to read for herself yet. She wants us to read to her.

You'll pardon my saying so, but the housework suffers as Joanne grows older. You can't stop your work as often as that child wants to hear a story. Why, you've got the garden and the chickens, the house, and that doll's quilt you insist on sewing for a child who doesn't even like her dolls.

I don't see why you couldn't just read to her in the time it would take to give her lessons.

Land sakes, Margaret. A stranger might think you never want the child to read!

Lillian's fan snapped furiously now. I tried to keep a calm expression on my face, but I could feel my lips tightening, so I pinched at the folds of the letter as if I could crimp it shut more tightly and silence Gar's voice on the pages, and handed it back to Lillian.

Perhaps you think I'm not the best teacher for her, she said.

Oh, honestly, I said and shook my head at her in open dismay.

My students still tell me they remember my lessons in the old schoolhouse. They wish their children could have had the same.

I stood up from my chair then, snatched open the screen, and said, You have my permission, Lillian. Good night.

But you don't truly approve, she said.

I closed the screen door quietly behind me and, standing in the doorway, I looked through it toward Lillian. She was waiting; she had stopped her rocking and even her fan lay still on her lap.

As you say, she's a bright child, I said and went upstairs. Through my open window I heard cicadas and the runners of Lillian's rocker that had started up again, chafing at the dark.

BY MORNING, the air inside the house was tolerable. At seven-thirty, Lillian and Joanne's ride was honking at the curb, and I stood and waved good-bye to them from the porch. I walked the mile downtown to Christ Presbyterian, and was sticky by the time I reached the church, although I'd allowed time to walk slowly. I sat alone in a pew and patted my face dry with my handkerchief. I had borrowed one of Lillian's collapsible fans, and I took it out to flick it quietly at my face. It was pale pink and stamped with oriental flowers that looked to me like peonies. It was one of the ones Gar had sent her from Hawaii when he first shipped out. The organist began to play, and I stood; the varnish on the pew back plucked at my cotton dress.

I was home again and standing at the kitchen sink when the front door's screen cracked shut behind Joanne. I sent her back to the door with a pointed finger.

Go hold the door for your Gran, please. The screen banged again behind Lillian.

Sit down, Lillian, I said. Your tea is on the table. I'm going to get Joanne out of her dress.

We're late, I know. We stayed for Benediction. Father Kelley left us no option. He said he was tired of seeing people leave simply because mass was over. It must be decidedly less trouble to be Presbyterian.

This was Lillian's way of apologizing for keeping me from my breakfast. I could have eaten before my own service, but waiting to eat with them was simpler than answering Joanne's questions about why God didn't mind Presbyterians having full stomachs before communion if he minded it in Catholics.

I fried an egg for each of us, and used Saturday's bread for toast. Lillian and I rubbed our plates clean with our bread, coaxed Joanne to eat up her egg, and I ate the last half of her toast.

Can I go outside now, Mom?

May I go outside, I corrected her.

No, child, Lillian said, Go up and get the book that's lying on my bureau.

Are you going to read, Gran?

I'm going to teach you to read for yourself.

I began to stack the dishes, but Lillian stopped me.

I'll see to the dishes later, Margaret, if we may have the kitchen.

Of course, Lillian. I put the plates down next to the sink. This is your house.

I knew the book Lillian had sent Joanne to fetch. It was a brittle old primer, likely the very one she'd used to teach Gar. I wondered if she was more anxious to see Joanne reading on her own or to remember her own past, when Garfield still fit on her lap and no one had thought yet of his having anything as inconvenient as a wife.

Joanne! Lillian called, standing at the bottom of the stairs, one hand on the newel post, the other on her hip. Bring the book and come down. You're going to learn your letters.

I know my letters, Gran, Joanne called down and began to sing: *a, b, c, d, e . . .*

Singing the alphabet is not reading it.

Lillian held out her hand, and led Joanne back into the kitchen. I stayed long enough once they were settled to see Joanne looking closely at Lillian, not watching her write out the letters on the piece of paper in front of her, but looking at her face, at her profile, at the white hair that rolled itself into a knot at the nape of Lillian's neck, puzzling her out.

Now sing your alphabet, Lillian said, sliding the paper closer to Joanne.

Joanne knelt on her chair and leaned forward on her elbows. She watched her grandmother's fingertip as she sang, rasping across the paper, pointing at its pen-drawn letters.

I went outside quietly and swept the back steps, flicking the dirt into the flower bed. The chickens scratched and gossiped in their wire pen; a thin breeze stirred the tomato plants and made the long curling leaves on the corn plants slap frailly at one another. Beads of sweat began to rise along my hairline and in the powder under my arms. I'd never changed out of my church dress, but I thought Lillian would want me farther away than I was from the kitchen door, so I took the small hoe and began to chop weeds at the garden's farthest end. I tossed the weeds onto the brick patch running down the center of the yard and stopped when I reached a morning glory with purple bells, snaked around a cornstalk. I twisted a leaf on the cornstalk and watched it swivel loose.

I'd seen the date on Garfield's letter last night, before I'd looked at the second page. I'd had a letter of my own, dated the day after Lillian's, which said nothing about reading lessons. I imagined the letter that Lillian would now write to Gar, complaining of my resistance, and knew that writing a letter of my own to complain about her was useless, because Gar would only remind me that his mother was Irish, and that the Irish like to embroider. I could have told him that I liked stories as much as anyone else, but had my limits when it came to putting in details that weren't there at the beginning. It was self-serving and immodest and, worst of all, neither of them seemed to care that it nettled me.

The sun caught my rings—the ring I had bought and the diamond wedding band from Gar—and I stood with my hand on the hoe, twisting them to bring out the colors. Mother hadn't had to pay for a thing for our wedding. Estelle and I had picked out the fabric for our dresses—yards and yards of watered silk, in ivory and pale green—and I'd paid a neighbor lady who was good with empire waists and leg-o-mutton sleeves to sew them. Garfield paid the priest something, I suppose, although he never said, and gave Estelle and me roses to carry on the day. I even paid for the food for our wedding breakfast.

When Estelle and Jack arrived that morning in their car, I had to wave them away from the church. Estelle stood there on the sidewalk, frowning at me, clearly wondering why on earth I was standing where I was and not inside the church. Neither of us wanted to shout, and finally I made as if I were just going over to greet her and walked across the grass.

What gives? she said. It's not off, is it?

I took hold of her wrist and flashed her an exasperated look.

No, I said. It's not in the church. It's over in the priests' house.

Whatever for? she said. She was instantly angry and looked past me at the other guests. I held tight to her wrist, as much to keep her from marching over to the priest as to settle myself.

Because I'm Protestant. They won't let him marry me in the church.

Oh, Sappo . . . She shook her head and took hold of my hand.

Don't make me cry, I whispered. It's all right, really it is.

Porter came over then, shook Jack's hand, and said, No second thoughts, Maggie?

I need your hankie, I said to Estelle, and I wiped my eyes quickly before I turned around to smile back at the guests and said, I forgot to warn Estelle about the church is all. I'm sorry, really I am. I squeezed her hand, and put my arm through Porter's.

Look at the two of you, he said, with a surprised, fond face.

Don't you start, I said, and I smiled at him with my chin high. Now, let's go give me away.

Garfield had been waiting inside. He'd missed the whole thing, and I decided I wouldn't tell him.

He was handsome, of course, standing there with his feet apart and his hands clasped in front of him. There was no hesitation in his face; he looked as if he owned the place. I breathed out when I saw him, and he smiled at me with his eyes in pleased anticipation. He knew the effect he had on me, with his wrestler's build and his black pomaded hair, and I knew without understanding exactly why that I had a similar effect on him. Men who looked and acted like Garfield Maguire usually went for Estelle, but I was the one walking toward him on Porter's arm, and Estelle, walking behind me, had surprised everyone by marrying a pleasant-looking man.

The wedding breakfast was at Mother's house, and she, mercifully, was kept busy with the food and our dozen guests, and only cried through our good-byes on the porch as everyone else laughed and waved me into Porter's car, with the *Just Married* sign he and Jack had tied to the fender and the string of tin cans hanging from the tailpipe. A passing car honked, and everyone standing on the porch and in the yard cheered. I stopped then and turned around to look at them all one last time. Porter wasn't standing with Frances anymore; he was standing with his arm around Estelle, squinting at me in the bright sunlight. They had both looked at me like that all through the breakfast, blinking each time I met their eyes as if they were just waking up and remembering to smile. I started toward them but Porter gave me a little smile and shook his head, nodding toward Garfield who was standing with the car door open, waiting to drive us across town to his mother's house, where I found my things unpacked and tidy in his room.

There was a terrible finality about standing there in his bedroom, the word *married* ringing in my skull. I had never known before that a person could be terrified and elated in the same moment. We ate our meal in almost complete silence that first evening, as if we had done exactly this many times before. And we had eaten together, the three of us, at that table before, but never with Garfield and me both panting to get behind his bedroom door and Lillian slipping prim forkfuls of dinner between her teeth, pretending not to notice. I scared myself each time I thought of what would happen in his bed, but I was curious, too. Kissing Garfield had been a revelation, not at all what I would have guessed from looking at him. Estelle had told stories of fellows with eight hands who seemed to want to siphon the life right out of you, and she had been relieved when I told her Garfield wasn't like that. He was insistent and tender, by turns or in the same moment, although I could never have explained how or in what measure. After Estelle and Jack were married, she turned to skimping on the details and gave me mysterious smiles instead and said, Just you wait . . . And then there was poor Lillian the next morning, pretending again that she didn't see us both wearing the same dopey smile when we came down for breakfast, fully man and wife.

I began to write Maguire when signing my name, and accustomed myself to hearing people around town referring to Gar as Doc. I was quiet when he worked on his patients in Lillian's front parlor, I learned not to worry when he came in white and shaking after extractions, and kept quiet whenever he wanted to lie on the davenport in between patients to nap. I talked myself out of minding when Garfield asked me to give up my job, and then again when we bought a car of our own and he didn't want me to drive it. I was pregnant six months after we were married, and had Joanne to keep me busy before and after Garfield was called up. I had waited years to be married, and now here I was again, waiting for Gar to come home from the war, for us to have a house of our own. I had learned to smile any time someone told me how lucky I was to have him stationed in a place as safe as Hawaii, when Hawaii only made me think of Japanese bombs.

Uprooting heresy in the celestial garden, Margaret?

Lillian was there, suddenly, standing on the steps with Joanne. I held my hand over my eyes to look at them.

Joanne would like to show you the results of her first lesson, Lillian said.

I followed Lillian back inside, so Joanne could read her letters for me. She read them backwards from *z* to prove it, hesitating only when the difference between *p* and *r* confused her. I reached for her when she was done and kissed her.

I don't know when I've seen a brighter child, Lillian said. She removed her spectacles to rub her eyes and the bridge of her nose.

Or one more eager to please, I said. I knew it was entirely possible that Joanne hadn't read the letters at all, but had simply memorized them backward instead in order to give Lillian the performance she wanted, but I didn't say so. Go on outside now, I said and shooed Joanne toward the door.

Lillian said, I'm going to lie down until our dinner. My brain is fit to burst.

Is there anything I can get for you?

Not a thing, Margaret. Except a cloth, perhaps, to tie my skull together.

Lillian appeared in the kitchen doorway the next day, too,

an hour or so before supper, standing there with her eyebrow arched and Joanne by the hand. I took my colander of beans and spent that hour outside on the back steps, listening to the lesson through the screen door.

What sound does b make?

Buh.

And how does l sound?

Luh. Luh.

Now read this word.

Buh-ail-luh.

Does that sound like a word you know?

No, Gran.

What do you see in the picture?

A ball.

That's right. Now read it again.

Ball.

The shadows were longer, and the breeze was finally coming cooler. Why anyone would choose to sit in a July kitchen when they could sit outside was beyond me. I smoothed my apron out across my lap, pulled a thread from the hem of my dress, and folded my hands around my knees. I tipped and tailed the last of my beans, digging my thumbnail into the ends that wouldn't snap. The small of my back ached from sitting so long on the step. I leaned forward with an elbow on my knees and combed through the beans absently with my other hand. I wished I'd gone out to the front porch by then, where I wouldn't have been able to hear Lillian and Joanne. I didn't see how her method of teaching was any better than anything I could have done myself. And more than that, it was clear that Joanne was resisting and that Lillian would never be dissuaded. Joanne would be reading on her own before her fourth birthday, come hell or high water.

Please stop that kicking. Don't you want to be able to read?

Yes, Gran.

Now this word, Joanne. What is this word?

Ball.

No, it is not. We already saw *ball* on the last page. What is this word?

Ball.

No. What is this letter, after the *b*?

That's *e*.

Very good. And so what is this word?

Ball.

I cannot abide willfulness, Joanne. You will stop your fooling, or you will not have your supper.

Bell.

Very good.

That evening, we sat in the yellow lamplight in Lillian's front room. I sat with Joanne on the davenport and read aloud from a book; Lillian watched us from her wing chair. At the end of the story when I closed the book, Lillian leaned forward, said, Come here, child, and opened the wide black album of photos she held on her lap.

Go on, I said, and Joanne went over and reached for the photos as if they were being given to her.

Don't touch. Lillian caught her hands mid-grab. Now, who do you think that is.

Joanne leaned on the arm of the chair. She shrugged.

That's your father when he was only a few years older than you are now. And that's your Aunt Helen, who lives in Florida, that's me, and that's Ruth. She would have been your aunt too, if she had lived.

I knew that photo well without getting up to see it again. Lillian and her children, arranged in a diamond: Lillian at the top, bent over an open book, and squinting without her spectacles;

Helen, tall and thin, her eyes wide open and snapping at some private mischief; Garfield turning to look at the camera, interrupted by the photographer; and Ruth, dark hair pulled back tight from a middle part, face forward and frowning.

Does she look like me?

Exactly like. Anyone would think this was a picture of you.

Why did she die? Joanne said.

Scarlet fever. She wasn't ours to keep. Lillian closed the album and stared at her hands spread flat on the cover. Now why do you suppose I wanted to show you that?

Joanne didn't answer, she was fixed on the album and knew that an answer wasn't required so much as the appearance of thinking.

To show you how I value reading. I was reading to the children in that photo, and I was the one who thought to take the picture that way. The photographer didn't want to do it. He thought we should just look at the camera, but I thought we should be reading.

Will you read me a story?

Your mother just read you one, and now it's your bedtime.

Go on upstairs, I said. Brush your teeth and I'll be right up.

I had taken up my knitting as I always did, rather than sit alone in a room with Lillian. Having the knitting to look at made listening to her that much easier and made it pointless for Lillian to try to examine me too closely. If I was quiet, it was only because I was concentrating. If I never looked up at her while she was speaking it was only because I had two, three, how many strands going there?

I was going at it fast, even for me, hoping she'd leave well enough alone and not say anything more about the picture. I hadn't liked seeing the looks on either of their faces when the album was open. Lillian smiling in a triumphant sort of way, pleased to have a new audience for her wisdom and her life's accumulated pain. It was Joanne who had alarmed me, though, and I could see that Lillian had sparked an idea in her head. I would never have dreamed that a three-year-old could look so suspicious, could wonder so clearly if she'd been duped. Not that it was a photo of her, and her grandmother was really her mother, but that she was Ruth come back by force of will alone, landing smack in the same house, in the very same family, but with a different name. But with Joanne out of the room, Lillian's focus shifted to me. I determined to keep knitting until Lillian fell asleep in her chair. She did so most evenings with whatever book she had been reading still in her lap, her head slumping forward, and her features swimming together in a frown. If I waited to go upstairs until she was fully asleep, I could tuck Joanne in by myself and try to set her straight about that picture. But Lillian surprised me. She wasn't sleepy at all, if anything, she was energized by her talk with Joanne.

I've annoyed you, Margaret, she said.

A person with her wits about her could have smiled lightly then, shaken her head, and said, Oh, no. Kept on at her work without even looking up. But Lillian was right: I was annoyed and couldn't pretend otherwise. I had believed my face to be a better mask than it was, and now there was nothing to do but meet her eye and answer.

It doesn't do to give a child notions, I said. Not when that child has a brain and an imagination like Joanne's.

I see, she said. But she didn't see. She didn't see anything of the sort. She was smiling at me, a tolerant smile that resided only in the corners of her mouth. She had annoyed me, and now she had provoked me to boot.

I didn't lose Joanne overnight. I let go by degrees.

·—*9*—·

J remember Joanne's face at rest. I see her face as it was
before it hardened or clouded over or did whatever it was
that she never retreated from, and it is smoother and more alive
than any other I've seen. I remember her cheeks, tight with smiling, and her laughing so hard she was shouting at a little dog she'd
just seen. The dog was jumping, trying to catch a bouncing ball,
and Joanne, new to walking, swayed on round legs that would
not yet obey her and bend or jump, so she clutched the front of
her dress, and bobbed her head to mimic the dog, instead.

I remember Joanne as a blur on the scooter Porter made for
her out of old roller skates and a wooden crate he'd knocked
apart. Forth and back! she'd say, and tell me how many times
she'd been from one end of our block to the other that morning.
And then suddenly, when she was seven, Garfield decided the
scooter was somehow a patchy disgrace, and he took her downtown to buy her a bicycle instead. Never mind there were still
shortages of everything after the war. Never mind that Lee was
in a navy blue snowsuit because there literally was no other, and
I'd had to tape a bow to her head to keep people from calling
her Buster. No, Garfield's mind was set on a bicycle for Joanne,
and so it suited him fine when all he could get was an outsized
bike that had no training wheels. He got on it to show her how
it was done, put her on and pushed her off a few times, and then

went back into the house and let her fight it out with the bike on her own for the rest of the afternoon. If I hadn't been away at Mother's that day, I would have held onto the seat and run behind her myself, or at least shamed Garfield into doing it, and Joanne would neither have put a dent in the front fender by crashing into a tree, nor would she have damaged both knees in learning how to ride it.

Gar was that proud when I got home from Mother's that afternoon, and he stood there on the walk with me while Joanne went up and down the block on the thing to show me. Imagine, Margaret, he said, she couldn't ride a bicycle at all when you left this morning. That put me in mind of Lillian and her reading, although I knew better by then than to ask what the hurry was or where he'd put the tin cup so I could drop a nickel in it. And when Joanne's legs were swollen the next morning and she could hardly walk, Garfield refused to see how it had anything to do with him and only said, One thing less to learn, my girl. And now you'll never forget it.

I know that the image of Garfield grinning like a fool with his hands on his hips while Joanne rolls by enrages me because of what it cost her later. I know now that a doctor told her when she was in college that her knees troubled her because of torn cartilage in both, and when had she done that? At the time, I only felt that I had missed out, as if she were still a baby and he'd coached her through her first steps and had her strolling before I got home. As if my contribution had ended with her birth.

Garfield dealt in absolutes. If you asked his opinion on something, you never heard him say, Well, now, let me think . . . He had his answers ready to hand, and you were never quite sure if he'd anticipated the question and had already done his thinking, or if he truly was just that quick. He answered even when there was something you wanted to ask but weren't bold enough to, and sometimes he told you things you didn't want or need to hear, simply because he wanted to say them. He saw a photo of Estelle before he met Estelle herself, tutted, shook his head and said, The curse of beauty. That won't end well. And then before I could finish my thought, he said, It was the way you entered the room, Margaret, that settled it for me. No fuss, no noise. You didn't need anyone's attention, you had nothing to hide.

The only way I could ever hold my own with Garfield was to say absolutely nothing at all. There was no point in engaging him, and I decided staying well out of it was my only weapon when his sister Helen told me he'd once added a long column of figures correctly in his head, beating the fellow with the adding machine who'd challenged him.

Even his recklessness was absolute. He told stories about his antics at the university that would simply have been far-fetched coming from anyone else, but that made him seem larger than life, even when the escapades were so reckless you listened half hoping he'd gotten what he deserved. Of course, he was still there to tell the stories, which meant he hadn't—he'd walked clear across town in his shirtsleeves one winter, just to see if he could do it, and never had so much as a sniffle afterward—and you were left frowning in dismay at the folly of it all, at his telling the story and laughing, when he should have been shaking his head, too, that he'd come through unscathed.

He delighted in the story of his tonsils and how he'd parted with them, and after I'd witnessed a few tellings I realized that the looks of horror he got were likely what he'd been after when he'd agreed to have them out in the first place. Fred, his college roommate and the top man on the football team, needed his out badly, but was scared, so Garfield told Fred he'd go along with him and have his out, too. The doctor performed the operations in his office, and the Lord only knows what he had on hand in the way of anesthetic, but when he was done he showed them the door and said, Now, you're both strapping young men. I don't want you coddling yourselves, and Garfield went home and drank a glass of grapefruit juice, ending from that moment any discussion of his mettle.

He was wonderful to look at, of course, which was part of the appeal of the stories, with that dark head of his, sleek like a sea lion's, and his eyes that went from blue to grey to green and back again, depending on his mood. He was no taller than average, and he had that bull neck, so you knew without being told that he'd been a wrestler in school. Even when he began to put on weight, he was always neat and groomed and the extra bulk suited him, somehow. Salesmen eyed me with polite suspicion whenever I went to buy his dress shirts, waiting for me to admit I was only joking when I told them his measurements. I refused, finally, to buy them anymore, and told Gar he could go in himself and prove that the shirts were for an actual man and not an escaped gorilla. He had a knowing way of squinting at everything and everybody that left you feeling as if he'd seen straight through you, a casual habit of leaning and watching, with his hat cocked forward and a hand on his hip, only sorry that all the other men were such sorry specimens, because where was the fun in an unmatched fight?

Another of Garfield's absolutes was that Joanne and Lee should never have a pet. Not just while they were children living under his roof. No, he was adamant and told them that if they were wise they'd never have a pet at all. They tried their best to cajole him. A fish? A bird in a cage that they kept clean? A rabbit would work, in a hutch outside. No, he was sorry, but he knew better than they. When I'd finally tired of their wheedling him and his politely ignoring them, I dropped a photo I'd found on the table between them of Garfield as a toddler with his old dog, Mike. Garfield, of course, never missed a beat. He wiped his mouth and laid his napkin on the table, cleared his throat, and said, Thank you, Margaret, as if I'd only done what he had asked.

Mike, he said, had been a mutt, and Garfield had loved him more than life. One day when he was at school, word spread in the schoolyard that the dalmatians that belonged to the Perkins family up on the hill had gotten loose somehow and were killing dogs in town. Garfield took off running, he said, didn't wait for permission, and ran home terrified out of his mind. He said that the gutters were full of dead and dying dogs and that he was sure he'd find Mike torn to ribbons, too. When he got home, the Perkins dogs were there in his yard with Mike. He paused here for effect, wiped his moustache again, and said, They were playing.

I rolled my eyes as high as they would go and then closed them, so I wouldn't have to see the look on Gar's face. There was a chance he'd made the whole thing up, but there was an equal chance that he was serious. When I opened my eyes again, I let one eyebrow drift heavenward to let him know that the playing dogs and the dying dogs didn't add up, and when he declined to answer, I wasn't surprised. He had his mother's talent for exaggeration, after all. If she started the day with a headache, it was a brain tumor by five o'clock. You're not Irish, he would have said if I'd questioned his storytelling. You wouldn't understand. Lee managed somehow to be dubious, and pressed him on the happy ending. He was way ahead of her, as usual though, and said, You're right, Mike didn't die that day, but I thought he had, so when he did finally die of old age, I'd lost him twice, you see.

As with his other rules and standards, Garfield's absolutes could be capricious, and he'd turn fickle when it suited him. Joanne and Lee were both diligent students and always got good marks, but if one of them came home with a report that wasn't all A's, she got sat on the davenport for a talking to. He never raised his voice, he simply explained over and over again how this was the sort of thing that followed a person for the rest of her life, and when they came home next time with straight A's, he'd sniff and say, That's just showing off. Get a B next time. Makes all the A's look better.

Garfield brooked no dissent. If he knew a thing, he knew it, and he dismissed all contradiction that did not derive from an expert source. I could never question him on dentistry, not even as he practiced it on our girls. I was not only not a dentist, I had only a high school diploma to my name. So he never asked my opinion when he put Joanne in his chair at the age of seven, filled her mouth with fluoride and walked away, saying, Don't swallow, that's poison. He told me about it after the fact, and I'd like to think I would have tried to stop him, or at least insist that he go about it differently, but the fact is, I've never gotten past my amazement that she resisted the urge to swallow for as long as he likely made her sit there.

After Garfield died and we needed a new dentist, the girls and I went to a fellow downtown who had been a year behind Garfield at the dental school. The first time he gave Joanne a checkup, he came out frowning and asked if Joanne had had a lot of trouble with her teeth. Oh no, I assured him. No, Garfield had always said that she had excellent teeth. He was still frowning, though, and so was I by then. Why did he ask, I wanted to know.

Some of the work . . . he said. He was agitated and avoiding my eye.

What's wrong with the work?

The work is flawless. You can't fault the work. He raised his head then, looked straight at me, and said, Some of it was certainly unnecessary.

Another person might have found a different dentist after that, but we kept going to him. He'd known Garfield, after all. He knew what kind of man he'd been and how that might explain what he'd seen in Joanne's mouth. Besides, I couldn't have stood the shame of hearing that my husband had used my child as a guinea pig from yet another man.

Near the end, Garfield and his absolutes began to slip a little. I tried to preserve his dignity and pretend not to notice, but he knew I heard him when he'd been drinking and was talking out loud instead of only to himself. I was drying the last of our dinner dishes one evening when he came into the kitchen and I realized that he'd gone to the pantry, but had never opened the door. He just stood there, staring at his hand on the doorknob and finally said, People respect me.

I didn't say anything. What could I have said? I just wiped the plates and put them back in the cabinet, and he went into the pantry and poured himself more wine.

He'd begun by then to see that his feet were made of clay. He never got further than being troubled by his persistent doubt, though, and he died before he could allow the painful admission that the respect people showed him was really only fear, but the sight of him there, stripped of his swagger and still shoring himself up, left me full of pity. And later that same evening, Joanne was all confusion when she found him lying on the davenport, drunk again on his jug wine, and he squinted up at her with the light from the floor lamp too much in his eyes and said, You'd look good in a sack.

How could she reconcile that muzzy figure with the father for whom nothing and no one were ever good enough, who had never before said anything more than, You look fine.

I couldn't explain it to her. He couldn't have explained it to himself.

·—10—·

They kept me from my mother when she was dying. She
was in the bed we'd brought down to her parlor once she
could no longer climb the stairs, and I was in a hospital bed across
town, birthing Lee. In my calmer moments I've wondered how
much, exactly, they all thought a twin bed with a frail old woman
in it might weigh. Was it truly so much that three or four healthy
adults couldn't lift and carry it close enough to the hall telephone
that one of them could then hold the receiver to Mother's ear?
And my bed was on wheels; there's no possible excuse there. The
hospital would have had a telephone somewhere, in an office or
in the hall, and getting me there in my bed would have been a
matter of pushing, not lifting at all. If they'd told me that Mother
was dying, I would have walked to the telephone between contractions, and asked for a chair once I got there. And then I could
have been helped back to my bed, where I could have howled
through the rest of the birth and spared everyone the trouble of
wondering if it was the birth or the death that was making me
scream.

When Garfield came the next morning, I took one look at his
expression and knew he was about to make me mad. I was feeding Lee when he came in. He pulled a straight-backed chair over
to the bed and sat down with his elbows on his knees, looking at
his hat in his hands.

Margaret, dear, he said. Your mother is gone.

He glanced up at me, but then went right back to staring at the lining of his hat. I cupped Lee's head in my palm. She was wide-eyed, watching me. I had been expecting Gar, hoping he would come before she finished feeding so I could show him how she stared at me, how good she was, not yet a day old, at taking the breast. My chin was quivering. I thought it was better for him that Lee was with me in the bed, that my hands were occupied in holding our new daughter. But I also believed that if I had thrown something at him—my pillow, a vase, anything at all—he wouldn't have flinched. He'd have let me strike him. Had they all drawn straws? I wondered. Or had he simply volunteered to be the one to tell me? It hardly mattered.

When, I said.

Last night.

When.

At a quarter to six.

Almost three hours before Lee was born.

Margaret, there was—

Don't, I said. I finally looked up at him. I can tell you the next thing you're going to say.

Justification upon justification came hurtling into my head: there would have been nothing I could have done, even if they had told me; it might have troubled my laboring if I'd known; my mother was insensible close to the end and wouldn't have understood who the voice on the telephone belonged to; they had enough to do with taking care of Joanne through it all. But who's to say if she'd have understood or not? Is it so unthinkable that the voice of your own child, your last baby, could drift down through the chaos of your dying and be a balm?

If Porter and Estelle had been a party to this, their excuse might simply have been confusion and bewilderment, their unwillingness to diminish the joy of Lee's birth, or the plain fact that, in arranging for me to speak to our mother on the telephone, one of them might be out of the room in the precise moment that she died. But it could have been heedlessness, as well, even if that flew in the face of all that I knew about them both, and Garfield and I both understood that it was easier for me to simply blame him.

We looked at each other candidly now. The balance had shifted; Garfield had unburdened himself and no longer looked delinquent. He was composed, his face was open, and I was left with the realization that there was nothing more to be said about this, nothing more that ever could be said. It was absolute. All that remained was for me to submit to the fact, to be able to look at Garfield, Porter, Estelle, and even Frances with something more than civility, because the very sight of them brought me back to my mother.

There are only two photographs of Mother's younger sister Nina as a child, as there are always fewer pictures of the youngest child, and I suppose my grandparents reasoned that the expense of having Mother and Ada photographed six times was fair because they were always photographed together: six portraits of twins being the equivalent of three individual pictures. I've always wondered, though, if they weren't simply astounded by how indistinguishable they truly were, and were making sure that there was proof. It's impossible to say which girl is which in any of these photos, unless you know that Emma Ada is always on the left, and Ada Emma is always on the right. They were never known to pull pranks on people that I've heard, the one pretending to be the other, but how anyone told them apart before they were old enough to speak is beyond me. I suppose my grandmother always laid them down and sat them in chairs the same way—Emma, left; Ada, right—but I'd have lived in terror that

I'd gotten it wrong one day and switched them, so that the girl on the left was actually always Ada after the one morning I was too sleepy or distracted to remember what I was doing. It's possible they lived in fear of that, themselves, and might explain why it was so easy for my father to get Mother's goat by calling her Ada. She never said as much, but it could be that Mother always wondered if she and her twin weren't living the other's life.

The last picture taken of Mother and Aunt Ada together, before they each married and left home, looks at first to be a picture of just one girl, staring off into the middle distance, leaning her temple against a mirror. It's Emma and Ada both, though; not just beside each other this time, but leaning their heads together as if to say, *This is the last time we'll be impossible to tell apart.* Once they were married, even if they still lived in the same city, they would no longer have identical dresses or be given identical jewelry. They would no longer get out of their bed in the morning and decide together how they would wear their hair that day. They became individuals only when they began to live away from one another, and the accumulated joys and sorrows of their lives could work individual tracks into each of their faces. But in this last double portrait, their dresses, even the drops in their ears, are still identical. They arrange their curls on opposite sides of their faces, lean their heads together, and hold still for the camera. *Not even we can tell us apart.*

Mother's courtship with Dad exists now in two letters. Just two letters out of everything Dad wrote to her, and nothing at all of what she must certainly have written to him. I found them after Estelle suggested I be the one to clear out Mother's closet and dresser drawers, as a salve, I suppose, to my feelings. The letters were in with a bunch of old photos in a hatbox on Mother's closet shelf, and when I saw what they were, I put them straight into my handbag without telling the others.

Both letters had lost their stamps—torn out of the corners and collected somewhere else—but the cancellations are dated September 1898 and April 1899. Seven months. The time required for the letters to progress from *Dear Friend* to *Dearest Emma*. The address on each is only *Miss Emma A. Stuver, City.* So ridiculously simple, and simpler still, there is no return address, because everyone in town would have known who it was who was courting Miss Emma, and where to return a letter, if one should go astray. It's on the back of the first letter, the one so formal it is almost stiff, that Mother wrote *Precious letters.*

He is no longer *sincerely* but *very devotedly* hers by the end of the second letter, although he still signs it Wm. Doud, as if they are contracting business, which, in a very literal sense, they are. He's away from home at a hotel in Topeka, traveling for the railroad. There's something wrong with his foot; he says he can hardly write for the pain of the hot poultice he has on it. *I shall be glad to get back to you again, should feel better if I were with you and could see you pass if I could not get out to be with you. It would be better than not to be able to see you at all.*

There's nothing else. Only a few pictures of them together, taken when they were old. They're not touching in any of them; they might look as if they'd each been cut out of another photo and pasted together, except that they're both standing on the same patchy expanse of grass, or in front of the same shadows falling across the same clapboards on the house. They stand slightly apart and at an angle to one another, Mother looking in one direction and Dad in the other, her line of sight crossing his. There is nothing to indicate what either one of them is thinking; they are just a man and a woman, holding a hat and a pocketbook, respectively, both posing for a moment, which is all right, but then they have to be on their way. They won't give anything away with a smile, and, besides, the sun is too strong in both pictures and they're trying not to squint. You have to remember their smiles on your own, and I do. Dad snaps his newspaper and grins, crosses his legs at the knee and bounces a slippered foot. Mother shakes her head at his teasing. Her eyes crinkle and she lifts a hand to her cheek and her smile is fond, as if it's Dad's hand resting there.

I knew enough of marriage by the time Lee was born to know that other things than smiles had passed between them. I knew from our Bible, although neither of them ever spoke of it, that there had been a son before Porter who'd died at birth. I knew that if their faces in photographs seemed expressionless, they were really only reserved. That if there were reasons beyond the simple fact of age for their gray hair and flagging jawlines, they were theirs alone to know.

After the nurses sent Garfield home that day, they didn't take Lee back to the nursery, but let me keep her in the bed beside me. That meant he'd told them about Mother, that everyone thought she'd be a comfort to me, and she was. I couldn't stop thinking about Mother, although I wanted to. I wanted to think about anything else than the last time we'd all been together at Porter's, and Frances had roasted a chicken for our supper. I had sat next to Mother and filled her plate for her. I knew she wouldn't want more than a few of the green beans and just a little of the wilted lettuce. I took a thigh for her when the bird went around and shredded the meat with my fork and took the bones onto my own plate. It was anyone's guess if she was following the conversation or not. Her teeth were all her own but they were unreliable, and she watched her plate and chewed so slowly you knew it hurt her to eat. She smiled and closed her eyes to say no when Frances asked if she wanted anything else. It was tiring enough to sit there at the table and lift her water glass. She certainly didn't need seconds.

Lee was staring at me again, staring as if I'd been talking out loud and she wanted to hear more. She fed until she dropped off and even after my nipple slipped out of her mouth, her lips worked at the air now and then, as if she still had ahold of it. I stroked her head and though she frowned a little, she never woke. I held my finger under her nose to feel her breathing, to feel her tiny bellows pull the chill air in and push it out again, warm and billowy. Mother had told me her own mother had done that when she thought Emma and Ada were asleep, checked to see if they were breathing. Mother had understood later that it was a practical measure—fearful, superstitious even—done to make sure the children would live through another night, but that she had found it so comforting she'd done it with us every night before she went to bed. I was awake most nights when she came in, and I suppose she knew that. I would lie looking at the light coming in under my door and listen to Mother and Dad talking, and then Mother would come in and stand for a moment beside my bed, my breath curling back off her finger back onto my lips. Sometimes I whispered good night as she turned, trying to make her stay, and she would bend and kiss my hair and whisper something so softly I couldn't understand before she left again and closed the door.

I began to fall asleep just after Lee woke and started to feed again. I wanted badly to watch her, because she was staring at me, learning me, but my fatigue after the birth and the news of my mother were nearly narcotic, and I fell deeply asleep wondering if we are only allowed so many family members at a time here on earth. It felt as if Mother was the price we had to pay for having Lee. Or rather, it felt as if Mother had known the price somehow and had left because Lee was arriving.

—11—

The bangle was in its box, at the back of my top bureau drawer. There were other boxes there with gifts that Mother and Dad had given me. Brooches, earrings, a broken compact that was too pretty to throw out. I hadn't taken the bangle out for years, not even to look at. There had been times I wanted to give it away, but there was no one I could have given it to without risking seeing them wearing it, and whenever I had considered it, something had stopped me and I'd put it back in the bureau.

Estelle knocked on my door, as I'd known she would. She'd been bursting all night. I shut the box back in the bureau and let her in.

I've never been so shocked in all my life, she said, and sat herself on my bed. I went around to get in the bed and shoved her over to make room for my legs. There was no point in pretending I didn't want to hear what had happened as badly as she wanted to tell it.

He was just standing there outside the fence, she said. He had his hands in his pockets, and he was looking at the house like it was a lion someone had dared him to pet. I saw him and went out to tell him supper was over, but that there was still hot soup if he wanted it. No preaching, just a meal. He took off his hat and came up the walk looking at his feet. He went right past me into the house, and I still didn't know it was him.

74

Estelle shook her head in fresh disbelief and said, I guess I started to wonder when he went straight to the kitchen like he knew where it was, but then Mother got hold of him and started fussing. Did he want milk or did he want a cup of tea? Would he eat a little bread and butter with his soup, and wasn't it a relief that cat was chalked on the fence so folks would know to knock if they needed hot food.

I'll never understand how I didn't know it was him, she said. He was just another man in an old suit, down on his luck and nerving himself up to knock on our door. I honestly don't know if Mother ever would have realized, and Byron would surely just have eaten the soup and left before he embarrassed her. I was leaning against the sink and studying him, and Mother was trying to catch my eye to get me to stop, and then it hit me and I slapped my leg and yelled, Byron Paine!

Shhhh! I scolded Estelle. Keep your voice down.

Imagine if it had been you who'd found him outside.

Well, at least I would have known who he was.

Yes, of course *you* would, she said. Let me tell you, you could have knocked Mother over with a feather. Why hadn't he said anything, she wanted to know. That's when I hollered that we hadn't given him a chance. The poor man had come here looking for Maggie and we'd poured soup down his throat.

Oh, Lord, no. You didn't! What did Mother say?

She snapped at me, but I wasn't having it. Byron wasn't saying anything for himself, so I decided to help him.

I cringed and my eyes squeezed shut, but Estelle didn't even see me. She was staring off at the window, so rapt with her own story it made me want to pull the covers up higher, as if she'd brought Byron himself right here into my room.

Estelle said, I sat down then and leaned in a little and said, Well, Byron? Did you come for my sister or the soup?

Estelle!

She looked at me and said, Wait'll you hear what he said: I suppose I came for the one and stayed for the other. Can you imagine?

What on earth?

I haven't any idea, but that was when I thought I'd better tell him you have a fellow.

Oh, Estelle.

Mother cut me off and asked if he was still at Schramm's, but he's not, poor man. He lost that job months ago and none of the other department stores are hiring floorwalkers, so he said he's been taking day jobs down at the depot.

And that's when I came in.

Yes, that's when you came in. With Garfield. Estelle was nearly purring from the pleasure of it all.

Go on, enjoy yourself.

Thank you, I think I will. She patted my hip hard. Oh, Sappo, don't look like that. Mother and Dad combined haven't given me the disapproving looks you have, and now for once it's you who's got man trouble and not me.

I had been paralyzed at the sight of Byron there in my mother's kitchen. I couldn't speak, not even when he smiled and said, simply in his deep odd voice, Hello, Maggie. I saw him decide to smile, decide to make light of it all when his eyes flicked over Garfield and then came back to me. But in that moment he first saw me, his face had been naked: half shame, half relief. I felt Garfield looking between us, waiting for the polite explanation that must follow awkwardness, and I fought hard to beat back the thrill I felt, standing there between the two of them, even as I also felt what had passed between them. It was easy to think that Garfield had the advantage, walking in with me as he did, but it wouldn't have mattered one jot if it had been the other way around and he'd been the one sitting. Byron was the slighter man in every way, a wiry accumulation of apology and doubt. Garfield would have eclipsed him in his sleep.

I heard Estelle making introductions, I saw the two of them shaking hands. Then Byron took up his hat and left, and I saw Garfield grin when Byron thanked Mother for the soup. I couldn't have said how much time had passed since I'd entered the room or how much longer Garfield sat there chatting with Mother and Estelle after Byron left. I couldn't have said anything at all.

I SAT out on the porch swing the next evening, looking up the street and down. I turned the silver bangle around and around my wrist. The houses were all quiet. The failing light had washed their white clapboards blue. I heard footsteps then, a man's heels striking the pavement. I waited until he'd passed the neighbor's house before I turned to smile. Byron paused before he swung open the wooden gate, looking down at the post.

They should have drawn three cats on that post, he said, grinning up at me.

Whatever for?

Three cats for three women. Three good women live here.

Don't tell Mother that, I said. I stopped the swing long enough for Byron to sit down, and said, She's so proud of that cat, I think she even chalked it back on herself after the last rainstorm.

We pushed the swing together. Immediately, I felt him struggling beside me, and knew that he still had not taught himself to speak when something was at stake, when there was something he needed to say.

How long has it been? I finally said. Five years? No, six?

Byron nodded in a way that told me he remembered the actual date, the last time in 1930 that he and I had seen each other.

We kept the swing going gently, as if that were the only reason we both were there. Here's the moment you risk making a fool of yourself, Byron, I thought. This is when you have to say the words, because we both know you've been saying them in your head.

You still have that, was all he managed to say, smiling down at the bracelet I was still turning on my wrist, and I nodded and smiled too. Neither of us heard Garfield coming.

Nice evening for the swing, he said, walking through the gate and up to the porch. He held a hand up to Byron. No, Paine. No, you sit. I'll be quite comfortable here. He laid his suit coat across one end of the porch rail and sat at the other end, one leg up on the rail, and leaned back against the corner post.

My mouth tightened at the sight of him, perched there like an enormous raven, puffed out chest and sleek black hair.

All done with dinner in there? Garfield said.

Dinner was over an hour ago, I said.

Garfield nodded slowly, still looking straight up the block. Looks like you and I have something in common, Paine.

I kept my eyes on my lap. I could feel Byron there beside me as if he were right up against me. His hair was as wiry and unruly as ever. I wondered why he sat fiddling with his hat and didn't just put it on.

Is that so.

Business is bad, Garfield said, then brushed at something on his knee, looked at me, and looked at Byron. From department stores to dentistry, business is bad.

I guess I get by, Byron said. I could imagine the proud smile he had forced, but I didn't dare to look.

Sure you do, a smart fellow like you. There are plenty of men out there who'd like work as day laborers. Now me, I don't see my patients these days until they're already in pretty bad shape.

I guess folks'd rather spend their money on food.

Garfield held up a finger and smiled. Yes, that's true, he said, but they still need their teeth to chew it with, don't they? You, for example. When was the last time a dentist looked at you?

I flashed my eyes at him in warning, but he stayed fixed on Byron.

You've got teeth, Paine, but little money. I've got time and precious few patients. What do you say? Garfield put both feet on the porch, turned to face the swing, and said, No charge for old friends of the family.

Byron hesitated. There was nothing I could say to help him, even if I'd known what that would be. Finally, he spoke, measuring out the slow words, I suppose that'd be all right.

Fine! That's fine. You come by and see me tomorrow, then.

We'd long since stopped the swing. I looked at Garfield's feet with my jaw clenched. Even when he was coming up the walk, Garfield would have seen clearly in our faces that Byron hadn't been brave, hadn't said the words he'd planned to say, hadn't managed not to fail. He could have touched his hat and sailed past us into the house with a howdy do and *You'll be in soon, won't you, Margaret*, but he'd stretched Byron out on the porch boards in front of me and made him bare his throat instead.

That's a pretty bangle, Margaret, Garfield said. My eyes fluttered up, but I didn't say a thing.

THE NEXT night, the air was cooler. There was no breeze, but I could still smell a change in the air. It was dark out, fully dark, by the time I was done with the supper dishes, and I turned off the living room lamps so the porch would be dark, too. I went out to sit on the swing and looked at the glass globes on the streetlights glowing yellow all up and down our street. The screen door opened behind me, and I turned to see Estelle standing there in the light of the doorway.

Come on out, I said over my shoulder. It feels a little like fall tonight.

Estelle stayed in the doorway. I heard her exhale. What are you doing? she said.

I'm sitting on the porch.

No, Sappo. I'm asking what you're playing at.

I turned again on the swing to look at her and said, Come over here where I can see you. What is it you want?

You've never had two fellows paying attention to you at the same time before.

No, but you could teach me a thing or two about that.

Estelle sat on the porch rail opposite me, instead of beside me on the swing. I thought she'd be staring at me, but when I looked up at her, she was looking down at the porch with a bitter little smile pinching her face.

She said, I know you think I have too many beaux, and maybe I do, but when I go with more than one fellow at a time, the one always knows about the others.

Just tell me what you're getting at.

I'm wondering if you know, exactly, who it is you're out here waiting for.

How is that any business of yours?

It isn't, really. It's yours. And Garfield's, and Byron's.

Byron's? Byron is an old friend, Estelle.

Oh, you don't have to explain it to me. It's nice, isn't it, wondering which one will show up first? Makes a girl feel pretty. Estelle turned to look over her shoulder and down the street. Her shoulders were hunched a little, her back bowed. She was elegant no matter how she sat, even when she was careless.

Margaret, do you want to marry Byron Paine?

How can you ask that?

It's only what Byron and Garfield are asking themselves right now.

It's been ages since Byron and I went together. He knows the situation.

All the same, he's yours. He's so desperately yours that he's hoping that pity will change into love. Margaret, I can hardly believe it, but you're being reckless. You have a care. Garfield will fight, but only so far, and then you'll lose him.

Since when do you think men are such precious commodities? Why, the stream of fellows going in and out of here for you should have worn a groove in the floor by now.

Yes, that's right, in and then out again, because I send them away before they can sniff out that there's nothing to stay for. If I had what you have—

What do I have that you don't have? You're the one with the blond curls, you're the beautiful sister. You're the charming one, too. I watch you with all the men who come through here, and I don't even mean your dates. I mean every last hobo who sees that cat on the fence and comes in looking for a meal and leaves eating out of your hand. You even charm the ones who blubber over their food. You make them laugh and feel like men again and like they might just be in love.

Sappo, don't. You won't hear me if you're angry.

Estelle waited for me to look at her again, for the hurt I wore on my face to soften. She smiled at me, and for a moment she looked exactly like Mother.

What you have is two men who see your particular beauty, she said. Two men who truly love you, not some idea they have of you.

My face crumpled then. Estelle sat beside me on the swing and pulled my head onto her shoulder. She laid her cheek against my head and said softly, Byron isn't a stray, Sappo. You don't owe him a thing.

But I do. I was careless with him. I knew that he loved me all those years ago and that I could never love him the same. I knew it and I pitied him for it.

Then be kind to him now and stop acting like you love him.

Is that what I've been doing? I exhaled and looked down at my hands. I suppose I have at that. I can't account for the way he makes me feel. It's confounding, knowing that he will never stop loving me. Not if I marry someone else, not even if I die. Garfield's not like that. He's not fragile. He'd never stay a widower, never treasure a hurt. Just like you.

Estelle swatted at me and laughed, I'm not even married yet, and you've got me widowed already.

What on earth do I do, Estelle?

You don't have to do a thing. Not if I know Garfield Maguire.

What do you mean?

I mean Byron sitting in that chair today and Gar filling his mouth with instruments before he laid out how things were going to be from now on.

Oh, Lord . . .

Yes, oh, Lord. And now that that's fixed, maybe you can stop acting like you think I don't love you.

I sat up, frowning at her, but she was still smiling.

When did you start calling me Sappo?

Heavens, I don't know. I've always called you Sappo.

What are you smiling like that for?

Because right now you look like you did when you were a girl. That frown. Just like in that photo Dad took of us here on the steps, only I suppose you were really only squinting then. She patted my knee and got up to go inside. Come inside and get a sweater. But don't lollygag, Garfield's bound to turn up soon.

He was there outside on the porch swing when I came back down, and said, Come sit with me, Margaret, before I'd even opened the screen. He held the swing still until I was sitting, and then we rocked it gently, just the littlest bit. An orange cat was lying on the cobbles on the other side of the street under the streetlight, feigning sleep, flicking up dust with the tip of its tail.

Tell me about the house plans again, I said.

The house?

Yes.

All right, the house. The house will be brick, with a red roof, and a big picture window on the front, and a fireplace—

And a dining room, I said.

If there's space after my office, Margaret, you shall have your dining room. We'll have a basement, too, and a garage, and a deep front yard.

I want lilacs, I said. And a crab apple.

They're messy, Garfield said.

No more than your magnolia.

Shhh, Margaret. Who's telling this? We'll have yew trees and redbuds in front, and a patch of tomatoes in the back. Garfield inhaled, relaxing, and moved his arm around my shoulders, but I leapt out of the swing and turned to face him.

Why did you do it? I said, my arms straight and my hands clenched.

Garfield stretched both arms out along the swing back and said, I thought one of us should.

And what if he should need something? He has no family. Where will he go?

Well, Margaret, assuming that you agree that he can't have you, there is nothing else here that he needs. Certainly not your mother's soup. If it's a meal he wants, he can go look for another damned cat scratched on another damned post. And if he wants conversation, he can wait for the tramps to light their cooking fires by the train tracks at night and take up with them.

I felt a wave of shock pass over my face that gave way to anger and said, I would never have dreamed you could be so cruel.

Cruel? I did him the great favor of his life by sending him away when you didn't have the heart to do it a second time. And do you know why? He stood up from the swing and took hold of my arms. He said, Because I knew that a man like that could never stand the pain of coming here each night, being near you, even touching you, and not having you.

Gar had me pressed against the porch rail. I turned my face away and said, I don't understand you at all.

He let go of my arms and stepped back, and then took my face in his hands and bent toward me. Yes, you understand me, he said. He kissed me slowly until he felt me relax, and then pulled away. And now you hate me a little, too. He went down the steps and looked back at me once before he went down the walk. But that's all right, Margaret, he said. That's all right.

I looked to see if anyone was in the living room before I went back inside, and then I ran straight to my room and got into bed without changing out of my clothes. I lay with my arms crossed over my face and wondered why I had waited, sitting there with Byron, for him to say that he still loved me, as if there had been any question of what I would say in return, as if anyone who saw us together wouldn't already know. I had sat there knowing that he'd pretended to himself that tenderness and love were the same and that the evening might not end with him standing up to wish me a happy life before he hurried out the gate. I could have decided for all of us by simply taking Byron's hand, and I did feel for a moment, sitting with him, that I could stay there in that moment of waiting, stay there in the forever of knowing what

Byron would say and pretending that there was more than one thing I could say in return.

There was no choice I could have made that night that was not somehow a mistake. I never thought any man would feel that way about me, let alone two, but walking away from both of them would only have been a different sort of mistake. I could have had no way, then, of knowing how much time I'd have to think about it afterward, by how many years I'd outlive them both. There was no way of guessing that Garfield and Byron would spend eternity pressed together in a photo album, two yellow strips of newspaper I still sometimes look at, side by side, to see how long I can stand it. I wasn't wrong to choose Garfield over Byron, but I was wrong in thinking that Garfield harassed poor Byron out the door only because he was fighting for me. I was the least of it. Byron and I were both innocents, and together we handed Garfield a first-class chance to be a bully.

I woke that night from dreaming about a sack of oranges Byron had once brought me. Smiling there on the front walk, he held out the sack and told me I was not to share, that they were for me alone, and as my mouth watered for the oranges, his face twisted into Garfield's grinning at me instead. Garfield took an orange from the sack, tossed it into the air and let it slap into his open palm, cackling at me and at the orange, slapping and slapping, until he dropped it and upended the sack and there was just the thud of oranges on the front walk until they had all rolled silently into the street.

12

J haven't set foot in Gar's light trap in thirty-five years. I don't know how I've managed to avoid it all this time. I suppose it just became part of the basement, like the boiler or the furnace. Something you look at but don't truly see, or even need to see. I never gave serious thought to taking it down, although Porter asked me more than once if I wanted to. He would have done it for me, I know. He would have brought a friend to help, dismantled it, and carted off every bit. I wouldn't have seen so much as a splinter go by, he would have been that discreet, but I always put him off for some reason. Thanked him and said maybe later. The last time he asked, I just smiled and shook my head, and then he stopped asking.

I had changed other things in the first years after Garfield died without admitting the one real reason I was changing them. It didn't seem to need explanation; to move a vase from one end of a shelf to the other made it my own. I was a widow now, and I need not consult anyone about anything. I had the davenport reupholstered and ordered new draperies for the living room. I swapped the painting that hung over the fireplace for the one that hung over the piano. Eventually, I even replaced the piano. I wiped every surface, cleaned every last thing.

When I brought boxes and suitcases up from the basement to stack in the waiting room and bought a bed and carpeting for the examination room, I told myself I was making the best use of the space. Joanne and Lee would each have their own bedroom now, and would be less at each other's throats. When I wrapped Gar's Army uniform in paper and laid it in the cedar chest and gave his everyday clothes to charity, I told myself I was making certain the house didn't turn into a museum.

I took down our conversation at the dinner table to practice my shorthand, and when that annoyed the girls into silence, I turned on the radio and took down the news, instead. I gave Lee Garfield's pocket watch and she timed me at the typewriter, and when I was satisfied with my speed, I went back to the electric company to get another job in the secretarial pool and needed no one's permission to do so.

When I sold Garfield's Ford and bought a used Dodge to replace it, I thought I was only asserting myself. The girls were aghast when I hauled up the garage door to show them, and, as if they had scolded me, I became indignant. I've been driving since before they had licenses, I said. Porter taught me. I even had a little Willys of my own before your father and I were married, did you know that? I sold it for parts, piece by piece, during the war.

I ordered them into the car then and drove downtown and across the river to Illinois and back to make my point and then, ashamed at having behaved like a child, I couldn't bring myself to tell them it was hardly their fault if they hadn't known their mother could drive and banged the door when I went into the house ahead of them. They each gave me that same look again when I changed the pictures hanging by the hall door. Garfield was gone, and in his place were their latest school portraits, colorized and framed. I simply pointed to the bookshelves by the fireplace so they could see I'd put him over there, or at least a smaller version of the same Army portrait so that he was with his beloved *Britannica*, still handsome and smirking, but that much further away.

We kept the beds made, the furniture and the windows polished. Joanne and I took turns mowing the lawn and we all raked leaves together. I hired a man to shape the yews, and another to plow the drive in winter. I kept Garfield's tomato patch along the sunny side of the garage, but expanded it to make it more my own, and planted tulip bulbs along the back of the house. Eventually, you could point to only a few objects that had been Garfield's, but he was still there in other ways: in the creaking of a basement step, in the turn of a window crank, or the weight of the air in a room, displaced by a closing door. The place was mine, but Garfield persisted, no matter how I tried to banish him.

I grew to believe privately that he was integral to the house as none of the rest of us were, as if he had somehow willed it into being, when I'd seen for myself the men we'd hired to build according to his plans. How Garfield would have relished my inability to dispel him. How he would have cackled at his own importance, elevated now and inescapable in death. He would have wanted me to laugh at the joke, too, and he'd have been right. It was all darkly funny, that he was now as unavoidable as the seasons, that somehow he would persist, even after my death, after the furnishings were removed and the deed renamed. Even when spring came and the same silky petals emerged from the low arms of the magnolia and lay too soon in rusting confusion on the ground, he would somehow be there in ways that I would not. And summer after summer would come with days of mayflies and sleepless nights of storm; thunder clapping louder than any Fourth of July, bedrooms flashing whiter than noon. Each year would wane, and his pear tree would drop its hard, inevitable fruit, and snow would pile again on the yews and the hedges, and Garfield would remain.

So I follow the flashlight into Gar's light trap and around the first corner, and I realize that I never let Porter take it down in deference to Gar, to his personality, his persistence, his force. If I never changed or even entered the light trap, it was a way of saying he'd won, and I realize as I'm about to turn the last corner, it was a way of giving Garfield's ghost a place to tinker, if he'd decided to stick around. I switch off my flashlight and step around the last corner, half expecting to see the red light on and Garfield there, bent over the sink. It's half expectation, half hope, I think, but it's black as pitch and I grope above my head for the light cord and yank on it because I've spooked myself, and that's when I finally laugh, because the light actually comes on. Thirty-five years and the damn thing still works.

The formulae (I had never said formulas again after the way Garfield corrected me) on the blackboard by the sink are still as fresh as if he'd written them and laid the chalk down a moment ago. I try the cord on the red bulb, and it works, too, so I switch off the white bulb and stand there in the red light as if Garfield has just gone upstairs to get another batch of films, as if he'll be right back, and then, when the basement door bangs open, I scream.

Melissa comes running down, making an awful racket, yelling, Damma! Oh, God—Damma! I pull myself around the corners of the light trap and laugh when I see her. That makes her mad, but the sight of her panting with her hand on her chest, exhaling and rolling her eyes at me in annoyance is too funny, and it's nervous laughter besides, although I can't tell her how glad I am to see her, how grateful I am that she's snapped me back to the present.

What are you doing down here? You scared me to death!

Good girl, I say. I didn't know if you'd find me down here.

What are you playing, hide and seek? Are you kidding me?

I thought you'd look for me outside.

In the snow, she says. She's looking at me as if I've just this moment lost my mind. You still have to get upstairs again, you know. Did you think about that?

No, I didn't, but now that you're here, you can help me up again.

She lifts a derisive brow. Do you have any idea how much trouble I'll be in if Mother finds out you came down here alone?

That's why neither one of us is going to tell her, I say. I have to stare her down now, appeal to her as a partner in crime and not as my jailer. It's exhilarating, knowing I've been reckless and that I owe her an apology because we're alone in the house, we're both in trouble, and it's my fault. I'm eighty-two and Melissa is twenty-five, but for just that instant I'm Maggie again, and it's Estelle there facing me, hands on her hips and furious because Mother left her in charge, which makes the candy dish in pieces on the floor between us her fault, too.

What is that? Melissa says, looking behind me. She's dropped her eyebrow and is on to the next thing.

It's your grandfather's light trap. He built it for developing his dental films.

What, like a darkroom?

Yes, but better. It's a maze, it was unique; something Garfield could feel superior about. Light can't go around corners. I gesture toward the entrance with my flashlight and say, Go on.

She flinches like I'm handing her two live snakes, but then she leans in a little and looks.

Go on. I'll go with you.

Of course that's exactly what Garfield said to me in 1950 when he'd finished the thing. Go on. I'll go with you. And I hand Melissa the flashlight and follow her in, just as he did with me. There's not really room for two, but then there's not that much to see, and when I've got the bulb switched on and she's flicked her eyes over everything, she looks at the chalkboard and says, Is that his writing? and I nod. She's got me smiling; Joanne would never have come in here with me, but then Joanne and I together wouldn't fit. Stay here, I say, and once I'm back outside the trap I call in to her, Now, turn off the light, but don't let go of the cord. I hear the click and I shine the flashlight straight into the entrance. Do you see anything?

Nothing! she calls back. Just black.

I go around the turns with the flashlight to get her, and she's got the bulb switched on again and is staring hard at the blackboard. I realize it's the first hard proof she has of him. I wouldn't blame her if she thought we'd made Garfield up. Just found a plausible photo in a junk shop and stuck it in the living room. Anything she knows about him, she's heard from Joanne. I never talk about him. I realize from the way she's staring at that board, though, that he's present for her as much as he is for me, but he's there in the silences; he's the powder keg, the elephant in every room.

I never tried to erase Garfield for my own sake; I did it for Joanne. And the harder I tried, the more he remained. The Lord only knows how it's twisted her inside, but the outward result was surely her hoarding. Collecting, she'd call it, because it's all heirlooms and antiques. She could fund an army if she sold it all. She doesn't get rid of a thing if there's somewhere she can keep it, but there's a haphazardness to it I don't understand, and not even Joanne knows what or where everything is anymore. She once bought an entire set of Spode at an estate sale simply because it was Estelle's pattern and she couldn't resist it, and then when Estelle died and left Joanne her china, she put it straight into the cabinet with the set she'd bought for herself, and the two were irretrievably mixed. People change the things they live with, she'd tell you. They leave their fingerprints on the surfaces, wear the edges down. I would have asked then why she'd mixed the china, why she'd jumbled Estelle in with a stranger, but she'd only have cried and told me I'd never understood her and she might partly have been right.

I had only wanted to spare Joanne, who would have seen Garfield's possessions as a rebuke, who could never have passed her father's hat on the shelf or his pocket watch on the bureau without letting each one become a mental scourge. She's managed it even with his things gone, of course. Stitched herself into an invisible hair shirt, and set about pickling herself with top-shelf scotch. Barring the hooch, she would have excelled as a medieval saint. And now I wonder how Melissa will make sense of it all. If she can ever comprehend the avalanche that's coming her way, or if she'll contrive by some miracle to sidestep it. That would be the thing, to step just far enough to the left that the whole miserable mess slides past you, but Melissa won't do that.

Once she's got me upstairs again and settled on the davenport, she can't stop herself looking at that photo of Gar on the shelf, and she can't quite look at me. Suddenly, I'm the elephant in the room.

She's right; I should help her, really. Point her toward things that will help her understand. She'll invent things if I don't help her, create a history that will make sense of her mother. But as soon as I've thought that far, I see Melissa trapped in a fright house, and each one of us is a leering jack-in-the-box, bobbing up at her on giant springs. The mirrors distort and every door opens onto a brick wall, like I've lured her into the light trap and taken away the bulb.

I see that what she wants is to understand, if not exactly to forgive, and I can stop it, I can stop it all from repeating itself. I can help Melissa to understand so that she won't be trapped and end up one day like Joanne did, aiming Garfield's voice in anger at her own child. Or I think I can, and that is the scourge I'll take for my forty lashes, because of what it will cost me to remember. Isn't that why I went into the light trap and let her find me there?

I suppose I had already decided that I would help her when I put the ring box in the pocket of my housecoat this morning, that I would provoke the right questions and let her ask them. I open the box and look once more at the diamond set in the table of onyx. I put it on one last time and remember, and then I snap it shut inside the box again and call to Melissa, Catch. It falls short, of course, and rolls to a stop in the middle of the room, and she laughs at me, Do the Cardinals know about you?

I flap a hand at her and shake my head. Oh, pish, I say.

She doesn't make a show of not understanding what I intend. She's seen the ring a million times before and now she's looking at it on her own hand. It fits perfectly, and that makes her look up and smile.

Garfield gave me that ring when your mother was born, I say.

She's grinning at me. We're conspirators. Mother's not going to like this, she says.

I shrug. She doesn't have to.

She's looking at the ring on her hand again, and that's fine with me because I want to look at her. Her head is tilted just so and she looks like me, like I did when I was twenty-five and had just met Garfield and the oval of my face was still lined with baby fat. I was closer to girlhood then than anything else, still closer to the girl with fallen-down socks and braids that slapped my shoulders when I skipped. Here I am, little Maggie, rumpled from playing and holding a fistful of cornflowers. And here I am again, stretched out with my woman's bones, staring out from my senior photo, all of eighteen, without a clue of what's to come. Now I'm a bride, looking pleased for once at what I see in my mirror; fingers skating over the first real silk I've ever worn and my coiled hair that's studded with rosebuds. Now I'm a wife, with my legs hooked around my husband's rocking haunches and my hand over his mouth so we won't be heard in his mother's house. Here I am a mother, lifting one child onto the toilet and coaxing the other into eating her bread crusts. Now I'm a widow, and the grass flies out of the mower the same for me, and I remember, by God, how to drive the car and type and do steno in an office downtown so I can put money in the bank and food on the table. And here I am, a grandmother, running my hands over the baby like I'm rubbing butter into a Christmas turkey, giving the baby my pinkie to grab and suck on because I've done this before and I know.

And here is that baby now, all grown with her woman's bones, twisting my ring on her finger. And I haven't a clue of what's to come for her, either, except for the certainty that it will surprise her.

13

*J*n the first weeks after Garfield died, I reentered my life with him each night in my dreams. I didn't dream about Garfield himself, only the work that had sprung up around him—the ashtrays and wineglasses that wanted soaking, the shirt collars that wanted scrubbing again—as if he were toying with me, keeping things running as they used to, if only during the hours that I was asleep. I dreamt of mundane things and woke each morning to find that everything was done because I had already done it. Things seemed to stay done, too, if only because there were suddenly fewer of them. I wondered how many hours I had squandered keeping entropy in check, how many hours were now left to me, to spend as I might choose.

I was baffled by my freedom. I didn't know how I should lie in our bed. I tried the middle for a while, but then went back to one side, leaving room for a husband, and stared at the shadow of the pear tree cast up on the ceiling by the post lamp in the yard. It was true that I'd had to take up work again in order to pay the bills and save enough to see the girls through college, but I didn't mind that; I'd worked before and I knew how to make money last. I was in no danger. I wouldn't lose the house; in fact, I never need move again. But I hadn't reckoned on proceeding without a husband, and it wasn't as simple as just keeping to the same plan but with fewer people. I didn't need Garfield to guide me, although a few well-intentioned friends suggested as much. I knew my own mind, and felt I'd deferred to him long enough. I was waiting to miss him, I realized, or waiting to admit that I didn't.

I was furious with him for dying. I still stand in front of his photograph on the shelf with my jaw clamped and my hands balled up in my pockets. Old age is not for sissies, I say to him. I guess you couldn't hack it. But wasn't it you who hated a coward? And then I remember his two sets of rules, and I remember the day Joanne found his violin in the basement and I had to tell her that, yes, he had studied for years, and yes, people who'd heard him play had said he was a fine violinist, and no, he never spoke of it himself except to say that he didn't want it mentioned. So now it's Joanne who won't play anymore, except at Christmas or when I insist, and she nearly stopped doing even that much the day I asked her why she wasn't using the pedals and she said she couldn't anymore and I told her that was nonsense, of course she could use the pedals, hadn't I paid for fourteen years of lessons so she could use the pedals, and she stomped off crying and hasn't touched my upright willingly since.

Garfield left me without company, too. I had thought that was part of the deal, having someone around, and his suddenly being gone felt like walking into the living room to find that the davenport had vanished. There were still chairs to sit on, to be sure; there was no need to stand. There was even the floor, if it came to that, but the floor and the chairs weren't what I had agreed to or what I'd come to expect. I might frown now at the hole my elbow is wearing in the davenport's armrest, I might worry at the way the springs bang each time my backside hits its accustomed spot, I might even look at the upholstery and shake my head at my own confounded taste, but it's mine and habit has to count for something. My davenport annoys me. Garfield annoyed me every other time he opened his mouth, but it beat starting over and I guess it beat being bored.

A person might argue that one of us had to go first, or even that my girls were still around so I wasn't alone, but children grow and children leave and I never married Garfield expecting to be widowed before the age of fifty. Gar might never have mellowed with time, but then again, he never even had the opportunity. He was cheated, I was cheated, and Joanne was certainly cheated. It can't be worth much of anything, telling a man who is already dead to go to hell, and I've no particular reason to think she's done even that. And I know it's contrary to chide a man for being dead and in the next breath to relish your freedom, to revel in the notion that there's suddenly more air circulating, just around you, and stifle the unseemly smiles that sidle onto your face because of the freedom or even the contrariness, because you're enjoying that one, too. Staying alive is the easiest thing in the world, I tell Garfield's photo. Look at me. I've been at it for more than eighty years.

Once I'd gotten a little used to widowhood, my mind turned to spinsters. I even wondered aloud once what my life would have been without Garfield and the girls, without any husband at all, and managed to horrify Estelle. I hadn't meant to say it out loud and didn't realize that I had until I saw her face. She took me literally, as usual, when even Joanne in the right mood might have remembered the figurative, the hypothetical. And I never said that my life would have been better, although I suppose it was implied that I believed it would have been easier.

I wasn't interested in imagining alternate outcomes for myself that in some way resembled the first. I couldn't allow myself to imagine having lived my life with Byron. The simple fact of my marrying him would have changed his life's choreography and saved him from that train, and although it might also have gotten him killed in the war, it might not, and he'd be beside me still, if we're going to take this to its obvious and ridiculous conclusion. And if we'd never had children, I'd have been another Estelle.

But I was imagining myself without any of it at all. No husband, no daughters. If I had never had them, I wanted to tell Estelle, I'd never have missed them. I might have looked at women who were mothers and felt that my life could have been fuller, but I wouldn't have been missing anyone in particular. Estelle only heard me wishing her nieces away.

Maybe I was being cavalier. After Barbara Jean had died, Porter and Frances never tried again for another child, so to Estelle my imagining myself as a spinster, even if only to imagine less housework, was as good as my robbing her of more of her relatives. And I could never have explained to Estelle what it felt like to have daughters, to feel that they had been with me all of my life, and that if they didn't figure in my early memories, it wasn't because they hadn't been born yet, they had simply been off somewhere else, as if out of sight in the next room. When I tried to reassure Estelle, when I said that I would never wish my girls away, she exhaled and frowned at me like I'd just come home hours after I'd said I would and she had been this close to calling the police. Well, I guess I couldn't understand her any better, really. Having that sort of power over a sister's happiness was not a thing I'd wished for.

It might amount to the same thing, but I hadn't wished Garfield away when he was alive so much as I often wished that he was different. I never held with divorce, and, thirty-five years on, I still use his name and sleep in his bed, so death didn't do much to sunder us. I did used to ask myself now and then whether I would still marry him if I'd only just met him, as a test of sorts, and it was abundantly clear to me that I would not. If I'd met him at thirty-five or forty, I would have viewed him as an attractive curiosity, but I'd have known him instantly for a caution. When

Estelle and my girls divorced, I thought the fresh shock I felt each time had only to do with their deciding that they preferred scandal and open shame to staying married. I'd never allowed myself to admire their nerve, and I certainly never imagined living to see so few precipices left from which a woman could fall: divorce, sex, even cohabitation becoming so banal as to make marriage seem the daring choice. I told myself I'd grown if I recognized my mistake, and that was the best I could expect.

The fact is I could have tolerated Garfield better as a pedant if he'd only left off being a bully. If he'd learned to be introspective instead of smug, he'd have suited me down to the ground. I liked his intellect fine. I even liked his always being right. He never understood, though, that a person can be smart and right without rubbing people's noses in it. He never even tried. I never dwelled too much on the things I liked about him. I suspected it was vanity that made me like them. *Look who I got! Look who the plain girl got!* I leaned against him in every photo, took hold of his hand or his arm, claiming him, displaying him, no matter his pose, which was sometimes so impassive I might have been a tourist posing with the statue of someone famous.

You can miss a thing about a person without missing that person entirely. I admitted only to myself that my kitchen felt empty without Garfield in it, leaning against the counter and giving me that eyes-only grin of his over the rim of a coffee cup that made me flush. Even Lee might still miss something of Barry, though I would never ask what and I didn't want to know. I hoped Joanne missed Stephen, and as little truck as I had with her divorcing him, I did admire her for carrying on. Stephen, for his part, did his bit and Melissa saw him each weekend, but he was able to start as close to scratch as a person could without losing his family entirely. He went to a new apartment with his own rooms, arranged as he himself decided. Joanne was fettered, not by

Melissa, but by having to keep things running more or less as they had for Melissa's sake. She chose to do it that way, but then she couldn't change so much as the silverware tray or the trash can in the bathroom or the pictures on the walls. Melissa got up from the same bed and left through the same door for the same school, and the things they'd agreed that Stephen would take with him—his books, the extra sofa from the guest room, the set of steak knives they'd gotten for Christmas—all left holes, and there was Joanne, left to fill them or to make it seem as if they'd never been there at all.

It felt no different to me, walking into that apartment, than it had before, and you half expected Joanne to say that Stephen had stepped out for a moment, that he'd be right back. But how it felt to her, I have no idea, and I could be getting it wrong. I had tried to erase Garfield, thinking I could spare Joanne, but had failed utterly at both the erasing and the sparing, and Joanne held on that much harder, determined to keep her bloody scourge. Garfield persisted, and it was all likely worse in the end because I had interfered than if I had just left his watch out on the dresser and his hat on the closet shelf.

But Stephen hadn't died, he'd just moved across town, and Joanne was able to flick the surfaces clean in a way that I was not. If something was missing from their home, Melissa would see it when she went to her father's for the weekend. A painting, a set of bowls, his row of pipes and his tobacco pouch. And now I realize this means that Joanne failed, too. She was fooling herself if she thought she'd filled in the gaps, that because she'd waved a wand and said Poof! everything was nice again. Joanne hadn't been fooled by my magic act—Father? What father?—any more than Missy was fooled by Joanne's. Their lives and their home were fragmented. Melissa was fragmented. She traveled by city bus to visit the pieces. She commuted each weekend between the halves of her self.

Our intentions were good, Joanne and I could both declare, even as we chose opposite things, but I wonder if she would admit that they were also selfish. I wonder if she would agree that we had both attempted a thing as implausible as frosting a cake and then scraping it clean with a garden rake.

·—14—·

It was Charlie Flodin who told me back in high school that I'd want to stop chewing gum if I knew how I looked when I chewed it. He said it after a basketball game when our boys had narrowly beaten the visitors from Brookfield. I realized years later when someone offered me a stick of gum that if we'd simply lost that game, I might have been more ladylike in my chewing that night, and would never have been compelled to give it up.

I was sweet on Charlie, of course, and it shamed me so to hear that I'd attracted his notice in that way, I could hardly look at him afterward. I didn't believe Estelle when she told me Charlie was sweet on me, too, but she insisted that he was.

How is it you think he noticed the gum, she wanted to know.

Because of the way I was chewing it, I said.

Isn't it more likely he saw you first and the gum second?

Not the way I was chewing it.

She wanted to shake me, I could tell, and she laughed and laughed.

Sappo . . . she said. You'd have me believe that of all the people in that gymnasium, with that game going on and all the cheering and screaming, Charlie Flodin clapped eyes on you because you were chewing gum with your mouth open?

I knew it was preposterous, but didn't yet see why and I was waiting for Estelle to commence teasing and wonder aloud how hard it would be to get used to calling me Maggie Flodin.

He was watching you instead of the game, she said.

Estelle had had to learn fast how to return or deflect the looks she got, because the kind of men who looked at her weren't generally the clumsy kind who later said the wrong thing. It never seemed that anyone looked at me, and if they did, I pulled at my hem or sucked my teeth to correct whatever it was I imagined was wrong and tried to think of other things.

I might never have realized that Byron Paine was stealing looks at me if Estelle hadn't told me to watch him. The railroad had only recently moved Dad up to Dalton when I first met Byron, and I met him through a girl I knew from the secretarial school, whose brother was his friend. We saw a good deal of each other at picnics and other socials, and though I never caught him staring, he did seem always to be on hand wherever I was, always seated next to or near me at tables, and finally I had to concede that Estelle was right.

Would I ever have noticed Byron if Estelle hadn't nudged me that way? He wasn't the kind of person you took note of, not right away at least, and if she'd kept silent he might have remained my friend's brother's friend, someone I had vaguely registered was about my height and had dark, unruly hair. It shames me to say it, but if I fell for Byron it was only insofar as I knew that he had fallen for me. He seemed to change by degrees, till he seemed lean rather than slight, and quietly wry rather than bashful. I told myself that the number of times he'd struck me as a turtle who'd misplaced his shell were not out of proportion to the number he'd made me laugh. His hair bothered me less when he wore a hat, and I liked the way he pushed his hats back a little on his head. He rolled his shirtsleeves up on warm days, and I liked that, too, and the look of his forearms and the realization that those muscles extended to his upper arms, his shoulders, and his chest.

How was I to resist, I'd like to know, a kind and tender man who wore his regard so openly? You might be persuaded you were falling in love if you laid your hand on a man's arm and felt the warmth of it on your palm long after you'd taken your hand away. You might wonder why you'd notice that his eyes were inky blue if you hadn't fallen already. But then you might notice that his smile was the fonder of the two, and then you'd feel a twinge each time he looked at you a particular way but then stopped himself from speaking because you knew what he wanted to say. You'd open your eyes when he was kissing you and close them quickly again when you saw that he was trembling, and then it would be too late. You'd hear yourself telling him that you couldn't see him anymore, and you'd fib and say that you didn't regret a moment of it, either, but then you'd always carry the picture of his face when he thought you'd left, when he thought you'd closed the door and could no longer see.

$\cdot-15-\cdot$

*A*fter Dad died, Porter helped us to miss him a little less, he'd grown so like him. It was tempting and altogether too easy to imagine they were two versions of the same person, although what made Estelle and me smile when we were with Porter might well have caused our mother pain. I'd seen Dad and Porter both, thin and leggy, standing so tall in their conductor's uniforms that any train on the track behind them seemed diminished. When I was a girl, I could look up at Dad, see his expression without understanding it, and know that the noise of the train was less frightening because of him. And when I first saw Porter in his own uniform with his own watch in his hand beside an immense and deafening train, I laughed because he was the image of Dad as a younger man, because he wore that same expression, and because I now understood that what I'd seen in Dad's face were barely suppressed elation and pride.

Once Porter had died, I felt useless for a while. Estelle was still around, but she was a thousand miles away in Denver, and after her I was the only one left of my generation. I began to sit alone in my kitchen at night. I listened to the refrigerator cycle on and off, I watched the moths outside trying to get at my fluorescent sink light until I grew sick of the small thud of their bodies on the glass, and I turned off the light and went to bed.

It was ridiculous that I should feel so adrift because Porter was gone, but I realized that in losing Porter I had finally, entirely, lost Dad. Porter had been Dad's proxy in so many ways, although I couldn't have said whether it was Porter or the rest of us who'd wanted it that way. It comforted us if Porter was there to do and say things as Dad would have done, but then it would have reassured Porter to know that he could comfort us. He gave me away at my wedding, and then gave my girls away in turn. I sometimes find it difficult to separate Dad and Porter in memories, I've superimposed them so completely.

I once found a dead bird on our lawn when I was a girl, and I sat crying over it on the front stoop until one of them, Porter or Dad, found me there and said quietly, Maggie, look at the bird. And when I looked down at the bird in my cupped hands, it was lying there with one eye open, looking back at me. It was only dazed, not dead, so I laid it in the grass where I'd found it and went inside to watch it from one of the windows that overlooked the porch and the yard, and when it righted itself and hopped around and then flew away, one of them, Porter or Dad, was there watching with me. I know better than to struggle with that memory and try to force it to let me see which one of them it was who was with me that day. It truly could have been either one of them, and if I'd had two such gentle men in my family, then I'd likely had my fair share.

I don't remember the first days after Porter died. Whatever got done, though, I did it. Estelle was home in Denver falling apart, because Porter followed so close on Frances it was all Estelle could do to fly in for the funeral and wobble on Harry's arm. That isn't fair, and Estelle would tell me so if she were standing here, but Estelle would never be dissuaded from her belief that we three would die in the order in which we'd been born, so if she shook for a solid week after Porter went, it was only because she believed that she was next. I told her every chance I got that she was being ridiculous, that she should ignore statistics and logic and even likelihood and remember that Frances had been three years younger than Porter, and by Estelle's own reckoning should have outlived him, even if Frances was Porter's wife and not a blood relation. That was impolitic of me and tantamount to telling Estelle she'd be a widow one day because Harry was a year younger than she was. We left Garfield out of it, because he'd died first of everybody, but then we left Garfield out of everything.

And then for years I couldn't think of Porter at all without remembering him first in his hospital bed. When his doctor told me it was his cigarettes that had landed him there, I threw my cigarettes, packaging and all, in the burn can that very day. I laughed and cried at the absurdity of it: four whole cartons of my Pall Malls going up at once, and me hanging over the burn can, sucking in my last official smoke like a character in some demented cartoon.

I felt it all slipping away after that. Even though I had paid attention, even though I had truly heard everyone who'd warned me *It goes so fast*, I began to feel as if every time I blinked I hurtled closer to the end. I closed my eyes and my husband was gone, I closed them again and my daughters were grown. Melissa, too, grown and gone, and I wondered if it was better to be able to say that you had been watching all along, that you hadn't missed a thing, or simply to realize that you'd been taken unawares and had arrived at the end.

I felt panicked, too, by the way our surnames had multiplied and changed through the years, as though it had left us fragmented somehow. I hadn't been in a roomful of Douds for years, and I was now the only Maguire for miles, because of a piece of paper I'd signed when I married Gar. I suppose Joanne and Lee could have gone back to Doud after their divorces if they'd

wanted to, but neither one of them did. Lee stayed a Cunning-
ham for reasons I'll never understand, Joanne went from Pierce
to Parker, and Estelle in her day had hurtled through both O'Dell
and Reynolds before she stopped at Lynch. I can look at both my
girls, peel back the layers, and know that they're as much Doud as
they are Maguire. I surprise myself and hope that Melissa never
changes her name. She'll bear a man's name either way. It might
as well be the one she grew up with.

I'd sit them all around my kitchen table if I could, the Douds.
Mother and Dad, Porter, Frances, and Estelle. Their oldest
selves, the day before each of them died. I don't imagine any of us
would need to say a thing. We'd just stare and smile, and I expect
I'd end up laughing because I'd be so much older than the rest of
them. Little Maggie Doud outlived and outaged them all.

But it wasn't any comfort to know that I was moving forward
if I was doing it alone, and I did feel alone once Estelle was gone,
too. No one had told me to expect that, and it didn't seem to matter that I had daughters and even a granddaughter for company.
As long as Porter or Estelle were alive, that little bit of me that
was Maggie was alive too, still the baby, still the youngest. I was
only Maggie, after all, I was just a girl, and no real use to anyone
younger than I was. I'd done everything I was supposed to do as
a wife and as a mother, and still I fell asleep each night staring at
the dark and wishing there were a grown-up in the next room. I
felt like one of those moths that sometimes gets caught inside the
house on summer nights and swims over the wrong side of the
kitchen window, but whether to find the way back out or only to
reach the light reflected in the glass, I could never decide.

I heard somewhere that true north changes over time. It
moves or slides, or some such thing. It eludes, and yet people
seem to navigate just the same. North is north, even if it's not
exactly where you thought you left it. You hold a compass out and

go where you mean to go, which must be how I kept moving forward with no one to guide me. I was Margaret, in spite of myself.

There was another bird one time, in Lillian's house, that I found in the living room one morning when someone had forgotten to close a window downstairs overnight. I knew better than to ask Garfield to help me, and simply went downstairs quietly when I was awake enough to understand what it was I was hearing. There were droppings here and there on the floor and the furniture. The bird had flown around for hours, too frightened and disoriented to find the window it had entered by, and so I opened all the windows and the door and sat down on the davenport to wait. The bird watched me from on top of a cabinet, high up near the ceiling, with its head cocked and its black eyes shining. We watched each other for the longest time, and then it burst away from the cabinet and flew straight out the window and into the open air as if it had known how all along.

—16—

The morning I lost the baby, there was blood on my underwear and in the toilet water, too. I pulled my nightgown
off over my head and held it up by the shoulders to look at it. There
was nothing there, so I put it back on and twisted the bunched-up
bottom into a knot at my waist. I knew that I must wash out the
blood and get myself new underwear, but I just sat and stared at
the blotch on the cotton stretched between my knees. Until I got
up, I thought, until I began to rub the blood away under the tap,
until one of the others woke and wanted an explanation, this all
still belonged to me.

After I'd cleaned myself, I took a towel from the linen closet
in the hall and then stopped in Joanne's doorway to listen to her
breathing. The curtains were stirring, and the air was coming
cooler now. I walked to the side of the bed, treading on the quiet
floorboards. Joanne's covers lay where I had left them, folded at
the foot of the bed. She was breathing open-mouthed, her arms
above her head on the pillow. I lifted a curl away from her cheek
and, when she did not rouse, I pulled loose the longer strands of
hair that had stuck against her neck.

I didn't want to go back to bed, so I lowered myself quietly
into the rocker beside Joanne's bed. I realized that I felt nothing,
and I was surprised. There was no pain, no cramping, no distress. I leaned my head back with my eyes closed, and the rocker

gave a creak that made Joanne startle and reach out her arms. I laid a hand on her chest until she settled. It was easy, there in her dark room, to remember her as an infant lying heavy in my arms for a feeding, pecking half asleep to find the nipple, pecking still even after she'd found it, and finally tugging as the painful cord of milk unfurled itself through my breast. No one knew how long I stayed with her after I'd fed her back to sleep, how I relished the middle of the night back then. There was so much to savor in the look and feel of her: the meaty hands, the fineness of her skull and brow, the rapidity of the line running from nose to lips to chin, even the sweat that rose on her head when she fed.

When I did return to bed, I lay down facing Gar with the towel folded under my hip and watched him sleep. I wondered how I would tell him about the blood, and how he would repeat it to Lillian. He began to draw a low rattling breath, and I let it grow louder without jostling him to make him turn over. I had told him once, while I had been pregnant with Joanne, that I sometimes watched him at night, and he had stared back at me sadly. But why should he be disappointed at fondness, I wondered, and why should I have been so bewildered those last months of waiting when the least gesture of his flooded me with tenderness? Hadn't I exasperated him with my crying when he had helped himself to a third serving of potatoes and gravy one night at dinner? It was only greediness, staying at the table after others were finished eating, but that night, for love of him and his helplessness around food, I had felt both pity and indulgence and had wanted to push the dish of potatoes up onto his plate and upend the gravy boat on the whole mess.

I turned away from Gar onto my other hip. I stared at the window and was surprised that I was sleepy. A trickle of blood left me. I reached down to push at the napkin and catch it.

When the pain came and woke me, it was beginning to be

light out. Garfield was breathing, steadily, deeply. The clock said five, still one hour till his alarm. The contractions were coming sharp and long now; I panted through them, clutching at the headboard. I remained silent through the pain, astonished that it should take so much to pass a ten-week-old fetus when my body had birthed one baby before.

I felt the towel under me, and it was wet. There was nothing to do but get up and put the towel and my nightgown to soak in the tub. I waited for the end of a contraction and walked, slow and bent, grabbing at the doorjamb when I felt myself beginning to fall. When my eyes opened again, I was looking at the bottom of the walnut dresser and the small porcelain wheels it rode upon. Garfield was shouting, Margaret! Margaret! and I heard Lillian's and Joanne's voices as well, but somehow could do nothing more than look at the dresser's wheels and the painted baseboards running along the floor.

Margaret, you fainted, Garfield said. Are you with us? Where is this blood coming from? Margaret!

I heard Joanne again, heard her crying, and I tried to lift my head, but then Garfield's voice came again and I closed my eyes.

Get her out of here, Mother. Go with your Gran, Joanne. Go.

She's lost the child, Garfield, Lillian said. My head was clear enough to hear that she was annoyed at the blood, at the unpleasantness of it all.

Go, Mother, Gar pleaded. Please go.

He put a pillow under my head before he went downstairs. I heard him speaking into the phone without hearing what he said, then his footsteps on the stairs again, taking them two at a time. I saw his face when he helped me up off the floor. I'd scared him and he hadn't had time to hide it.

Doc Gower is coming in a little while, he said. Let's get you to the bathroom.

I heard him pacing outside the door while I cleaned myself and changed, and when he heard me put the stopper in the tub and begin to run water over my nightgown and the towel, he called out, Leave them, I'll take care of them. He walked me back to the bed with his arm around my waist and I laid down on a fresh towel he'd put there for me. He stood there then, beside the bed with his hands on his hips, looking down at the quilt as if he wanted to say something, but then he simply exhaled and went downstairs to wait.

The contractions began to lessen soon after, and I went to the bathroom to see if the bleeding had stopped. I stood raised half up above the toilet and saw that the water was still bloody, but then sat again when I felt something leaving me and reached down quick to catch it. My fingers were bloodied, cupped around a little wet lump. I wrapped it quickly in toilet paper, over and over, washed the blood off my hands, and hid the bundle in my hand when I left the bathroom.

Margaret, is that you? Garfield called from downstairs. Please wait for me to help you. His voice was irritated.

I hurried. He was coming again. I wrapped the bundle in a hankie from my top drawer, put it in the empty ring box I had there, and stuffed it beneath the pile of my underthings just as Garfield appeared in the doorway.

I was just getting a hankie, I said, pushing the drawer shut again and holding an ironed square of cotton out on my palm to show him.

Look at you, he said. You're white as a sheet. Please don't get out of bed without my help. Mother and I will have enough to do without worrying about your fainting again.

I don't feel faint anymore, I said.

Please, Margaret. People don't usually know they're going to faint before they do.

He wouldn't leave until I was lying in bed again, staring at the title page of the book he brought up for me to read. Joanne appeared once he was gone, and ran to the bed when I stretched out my arm to her.

When did you get so big? I whispered into her hair. Before I could even take in the smell of her head, Lillian was there in the doorway.

There you are, Joanne, she said. Come with Gran now and leave your mother be.

Oh, for pity's sake, she's fine. She's all the medicine I need.

Joanne pulled my face against hers as she often did, so that her chin was pressing into the bridge of my nose. She pulled hard, until it hurt, as if she were trying to get inside me somehow. I usually chided her for it, for the pain, but now with Lillian watching us I only wondered how long she would bear down on me before she finally stopped on her own.

Careful, child! Lillian scolded. Now come with Gran.

She led Joanne away, and returned alone with the small electric fan, which she set on a table and aimed at my face.

I'll get a dish of ice to put in front of that fan later on after lunch. What else do you need, Margaret?

Not a thing, I said. Thank you. I'd get what I needed myself, I thought, if you two would only let me. Only the more Lillian had to do for me now, the better the story would be later, down at the beauty parlor.

The things you left in the tub are clean, Lillian said. She pushed her balled-up hands into the pockets of her housecoat. They all came clean.

There was something in her face, an unguarded flash I couldn't make out before it was gone.

I wish I could have done that, I said.

Well, you couldn't. You need to rest, and that's that.

Where's Joanne?

You needn't worry about her. She's with Garfield.

Land sakes, I wasn't worried. You two needn't work so hard to keep her away from me, either.

Lillian stood there still, pushing her fists harder into her pockets until her housecoat began to ride up in back.

What is it? I finally asked, since Lillian was never one to linger.

She forced her eyes up off the floor to say her piece. You won't understand this yet, she said, but if you had to lose this child, it's a good thing you lost it now, early. God has spared you considerable pain.

I stared back at her, dumbfounded. Normally, I would have looked away, embarrassed, but now I could only stare. I should have seen it coming, I thought. I should have guessed that Lillian would invoke Ruth, her own dead child, while I was in the middle of losing my own. A shocked laugh burst out of me.

I can see that you don't agree.

Oh, no. I would never compare this to your losing Ruth. I spoke slowly, knowing that Lillian would never have dared to have this conversation with me if Garfield had been in the room.

Lillian's shoulders lowered, she lifted her chin.

I only wonder why you would, I said.

Lillian looked out the two open windows.

There's a storm coming, she said finally, with a forced lightness in her voice. Maybe we'll get some relief from this heat tonight.

We can use the rain, I said, but it won't change a thing.

If there's nothing else you need, I'd better get out and burn the trash while there's time.

Thank you, not a thing.

I looked back at the book in my hands without really seeing it, relieved that we had gone back so quickly to our customary politenesses, but after Lillian had gone I frowned and looked at the door. There was no trash to burn, I thought. I burned what there was only yesterday.

I heard the screen door bang shut in the kitchen, and then everything was still. I got quietly out of bed and went to the hall window overlooking the back yard and, standing out of sight, watched Lillian empty the bathroom garbage into the burn can. My soiled napkins, wrapped in toilet paper, my bloodied towel and nightgown, all stuffed in with wads of newspaper around them. Lillian dropped in the lit matches and replaced the lid. She looked up at the house quickly, furtively, and I stepped back from the window.

The screen door opened and banged shut again, and I went back to bed, knowing I was expected to be there. I wanted the ring box, but the drawer was noisy and would have given me away. I stared at the dresser instead, astonished that it contained all that was left of a child. That and the stuff still seeping out of me.

I suppose that was one way to get everything clean, I said to myself and turned my eyes away.

A WEEK later, I told Garfield I wanted to take the zinnias I'd started to plant at Mother and Dad's graves. I said this knowing that he would insist on driving, and I kept my voice light.

You weren't thinking of walking, he said.

No, Gar, I wasn't.

Are you sure this won't be too much for you? Maybe I could drive Mother over with the flowers instead.

It's been a week, I said, and I feel fine. I will plant my own flowers myself, thank you very much.

All right, Margaret. As you wish.

Lillian was out of the house at her Ladies' Guild meeting, and with her gone I knew I'd get to the cemetery with that much less sparring. Garfield was mollifying me and thinking himself indulgent, but I found that those things stung a little less if I expected them both.

I sat in the car with the box of flowers on my lap to hide the bulge the ring box made in my dress pocket. I felt the box pressing against me through my dress and wanted to put my hand in the pocket to hold it so badly I wondered that I didn't cry out.

Garfield parked the car in a shady spot on the drive that wound through the cemetery.

Shall I come with you?

No, I said. I remembered to modulate my voice. Thank you, but I won't be long.

I almost stopped, thinking I was being ungenerous, that my miscarrying was a loss to him, too, and that he might have thought that visiting a family grave—any family grave—would be a consolation, but just as quickly I got out of the car alone and walked over the grass to the graves and knelt with my back to him on a folded newspaper I put down a little ways back from the headstones. There was precious little I could call my own, and I was not prepared to give this up. I dug a hole with my trowel, much deeper than the flowers required, and stopped to take off my gardening gloves. I waited then, to listen without turning around, and when I heard nothing more than leaves in the breeze, I took the ring box out of my pocket. I opened it and touched my lips to the wadded handkerchief inside in a movement swift enough that Garfield would think I was only brushing something from the tip of my nose. I was sure he was watching me, the way he and Lillian had both been watching me these last days, unwilling or unable to concede that it was only grief that had made me peculiar.

I couldn't put the ring box in the ground. I squeezed it with both hands, tight against my belly. My chest began to heave, and I stifled a moan, but even my clenched jaw couldn't keep it from becoming a lament, high pitched and keening. I realized I was bent over, pulling the box into my belly like a knife, and then I hurried, fearful of Gar finding out what I was holding, and I loosened my grip, set the ring box into the hole and covered it with dirt, tipping the flowers out of their pots to plant quickly on top of it.

When I returned to the car, Garfield asked, Why didn't you wear your gardening gloves? You could have kept your hands clean.

I turned away toward the window to hide my face and watch the rows of headstones curving away from us as we drove toward the front gate.

I can wash my hands at home, can't I, I said. You needn't drive me next time. I believe I'll be strong enough to walk by then.

That night, while Garfield was sleeping, I lay facing away from him, watching the curtains blow lightly into the room, then collapse against the window screen. The air was cool, finally, and damp. I thought of the ring box that, even in the ground, was still mine. There had been no blood to explain, no sheets to burn. It was little enough; I wouldn't share it.

I covered myself with the heavy cotton sheet and pressed my fist into my belly with my body curled around it. My mouth opened wide as if to howl, and I pressed the sheet over it.

I want, I whispered.

I want.

It's easy to pick out the bad things, of course. They stay with you. But it seems a worse thing to be reminded of something you'd thought was forgotten and see it perpetuated and reenacted by the next generation. It was one thing to sit with Joanne in front of the picture window, looking at the birds that came to the feeder in the pear tree, and listen to Garfield hold forth about each one's virtues and defects, to hear him deride the cardinals for being merely pretty, and praise the blue jays, who were handsome birds and bold besides, and it was something else again to later hear Joanne tell Melissa that she was wrong about my crows, that they couldn't be her favorite bird because their voices were ugly.

I had preferred the cardinals to the jays, but that was wrong. A blue jay is a bird you can admire, Garfield said. They're forceful, never cowardly.

They're bullies, I said.

Perhaps, he said.

Garfield was nothing more than a blue jay, himself. The bully who blinds you with his plumage, who gets what he wants and tells you what to think while he's getting it. Why on earth shouldn't a child love a crow for its squawk? Why shouldn't the commonplace be the thing that beguiles? When Melissa was small, she loved dandelions, and the cornflowers that grew

119

everywhere in summer, but Joanne sniffed. Weeds, she said, and Melissa learned to keep her thoughts to herself.

If I'd had my wits about me that first day, I'd have reminded Garfield that there was no bird I resembled so much as the cardinal, the small brown female whose plainness is her virtue. We were that far-fetched as a pair, Garfield and I. The dazzling bird alights and rides the slow bounce of the branch, the dun female stands behind the foliage, the intimation of red betrays her, and the blue head turns.

No one ever needed to think a thought around Garfield; he would think them for you. You needn't ever wonder about anything, either, or cultivate opinions or judgments. He'd cheerfully set you straight. Pointing out weakness where he saw it was an indoor sport, and Garfield construed fine qualities like kindness or caution as weakness when and where it suited him. He felt entitled to do it, somehow, and if you didn't agree that he was doing you a service, that was all right; he knew he was, and that was good enough for the both of you for now. Weakness of character, spinelessness he would have called it, galled him most, and he laughed at the dinner table when he told about the big men who soaked their shirts in his chair, whose chests he had to lean on to hold them down through their extractions, calling them craven instead of merely fearful.

He'd say, Give me a little old lady any day, or better yet, my own daughter. She has the sense to grip the chair arms and keep quiet while I work. But he was as wrong about them as he was about the men. There was little he could do to his elderly ladies that life had not already done; his pliers and his drill did not impress. And if he'd once looked into Joanne's eyes instead of in her mouth, he'd have seen with painful clarity that the pluck he liked to crow about was all a sham.

I don't know if Garfield deceived anyone as long or as well

as he deceived himself. In this, I've always thought that being a Catholic did him harm. He was too inclined to do and say as he liked, knowing that he could ask forgiveness in the priest's box. He went to St. Paul's each Sunday, and he took care of the priests' and the nuns' teeth, and if anything and everything could be forgiven, whatever was the point in behaving? He never learned the trick of introspection, of self-censure as a way to grace. He claimed it was only devilry, and though he knew better than to attempt most of it with me, my disapproval and bafflement never seemed to matter. I couldn't understand it, when he had everything a man could want. Looks and brilliance and a family and letters following his name, and still he could never resist taking other men by the arm, even men who had less, and twisting until they began to bend and twisting still with a smile as they crumpled and then holding on when they were on their knees and smiling down at them as if he'd done them a favor and asking, How's the weather down there?

He'd become estranged from his sister Helen precisely because he'd bullied her when Lillian died, saying he should have the lion's share of the estate because Helen's husband had no siblings and stood to inherit from his family alone. And I never could fault Helen there. It wasn't the idea itself so much as it was the high-handed way he put it to her. She and her family were already living in Florida by then; it was easy for her to tell him to go to hell and walk away with her half of the estate. We didn't see her again until Gar's funeral, and I never saw her after that. She and I sent Christmas cards and the odd snapshot. We could have visited, but the distance was too great and though we had our memories of Garfield in common, that was too sour a thing to rebuild upon. Besides, I wanted my girls to feel that, despite the evidence of their surname, they belonged more to the Douds than the Maguires. I had no desire to cultivate what remained of Garfield's blood relations.

It always seemed to me to be a waste of intelligence, a pitiful waste, to have a mind like Gar's but no talent or desire for self-scrutiny. He couldn't see himself for what he was any more than he could see how others saw him, and who can say which is worse or if they are really different things at all.

When he was stationed in Hawaii during the war, Joanne forgot him. He was the soldier with the moustache who, as far as she could see, did nothing more than sit the war out in a frame on a table in Lillian's front room. She kissed his picture every evening when Lillian told her, Say good night to Daddy Gar. And even when he had come home, she went straight to his photograph that first night to kiss it and made Garfield laugh. He leaned forward with his arms out to her and told her, Here I am! And she looked at him and the photograph and then at me, and only when I nodded would she go to him.

She had been wary at the depot when we went to meet him, but I'd expected that. Lillian told her she had known her father before the war and she would know him still, and Joanne stood between us, holding our hands as we watched the men pour off the train. We were crying before we saw him, Lillian and I, and then he was there, he'd picked us out in the crowd and stood there a moment watching. I crouched down and pointed. There he is! And then he was right in front of me, taking off his hat, kissing his mother, kissing me. Joanne must have been looking up at us all, waiting for it to make sense, to remember how the word *father* should feel in her mouth, waiting to believe that she was doing something more than pretending. She blurted it out—Welcome home, Daddy Gar—the words she had practiced, that we'd told her would be her gift to him, and then she cried when he picked her up to kiss her. He laughed, of course, we likely all did, and kissed her again even as she arched away from him and reached for me.

I knew she'd recognize me, he said, and I thought that he

was joking. He'd become a stranger to his small daughter, and I thought for days that he had been making light of having to resume as if they'd never met before. But he never tried to win her away from her skepticism; he never wooed her, he simply began where he had left off, imperious and exacting, and if she was quickly persuaded that he was her father, it was only because the alternative, that I would allow a man like him in the house for any other reason, was unthinkable. And in all these years I have still not convinced myself, one way or the other, whether he believed that Joanne recognized him that day or if he was bluffing, and whether I should be ashamed of him for thinking himself indelible, or merely pity him for wishing it were so.

·—18—·

elissa told me once that we make up our memories. I take an image of her and another of the way my Christmas tree always looks and put them on top of my living room, and even if I'm convinced I've just remembered Melissa a year ago at Christmas, I haven't; I've made the whole thing up. She had it in a psychology course, she said, and I'm inclined to believe her, if only because I've never known Missy to use her brain as a cudgel. She's respectful, and she can tell you a thing without looking dismayed, without looking disappointed that you hadn't known it before. Recollect was the word Melissa used. We collect and re-collect images and then piece them together. Joanne would only have been provoked if she'd heard that one. She can't abide an unorthodox thought. She would have gone off on one of her tirades about Latin and Greek roots until she'd buried Melissa's original point. But Melissa didn't tell her mother, she told me.

That one, I tell Missy, pointing at the shelf.

This one here? She's already pulling it out from the pile, but I stop her and say, No, the one below it. Oh, just take them all down.

They're dusty, all of them, all the hatboxes and albums she's stacked on the floor. She smiles and nods when I say, You couldn't get a damp cloth, could you? And when we're sitting on the davenport and the album that I wanted is open on my lap, Melissa stares at the photographs as if she'd like to find a way to climb into them. I try to look at them like I don't have anything particular in mind. In fact, I'm not at all sure what I intend, and I'm hoping the pictures will tell me. I turn a page or two and stop. That's your mother, I say. She would have been about six there.

Joanne is dressed in a striped shirt and dungarees, wearing her cowboy hat and her little cowboy boots. Garfield is beside her with another of Joanne's hats, a little straw one, perched on his head. He's sitting on Lillian's front stoop with his arm around Joanne, and she's got one arm around his neck. They're both squinting in the sunlight a little, smiling for me and the camera. When Joanne had put that other hat on his head, I'd told them both to wait a minute, I'd be right back, and I went and got the camera because I wanted a picture of Garfield looking like any other father, like a man smiling for the silliness of the too-small hat and the feel of his daughter's puppy-round belly under his hand.

No, no, I thought. This won't do. That picture might tell the truth of that moment, but it doesn't tell the truth, and I start turning pages, but Melissa stops me. Where was this taken? she wants to know and she takes the album onto her lap.

San Francisco, I say. Garfield was shipping out to Hawaii, and I went out on the train to see him off.

This one won't do, either. Garfield looks too fine in his uniform, and I'm holding tight to his arm, holding Garfield like I've won him as a prize. I'm smiling wide for the camera. I've forgotten my teeth entirely and I'm smiling like a lunatic for a stranger I've given our camera to in a city I'd never visited before and haven't been to since. I was hoping to find one of the pictures of Garfield and me where it looks like he's doing me a favor, standing there with me. I know there's a picture where I'm trying to hold his hand and he won't hold mine, and another where I've put my arm through his and he hasn't so much as bent his arm at the elbow to suggest that he gave it to me to take. I lift the remaining pages of the album instead, to get at the two clippings at the back.

It chagrins me, each time I'm reminded that I've kept these clippings together, when I could easily have put Garfield in one album and Byron in another. But just the same, I know my reasons for doing so have only to do with Garfield and with the way he handed me the newspaper that day, already open to the right page, with not so much as a by the by to warn me first that Byron was dead, that he'd come home from the war only to be struck by a train. And there I was, reading the news with Garfield beside me, fiddling with something he'd gotten out of a drawer while he waited to see my reaction. They'd run Byron's army photo with the obituary, and in it he wore a look of pleasant surprise, as if things were going fairly well and he hoped they'd continue that way. It was an expression I remembered because it was one he had tried always to maintain, even when things were going poorly. And when things did go poorly, as they often did with Byron, that expression teetered between contentment and weeping because he was seemingly helpless to act upon events, and would simply freeze. That was how he'd lost his fight with Garfield and found himself in the dental chair, and although it was sad, it wasn't a stretch to imagine it was how he'd gotten stuck in front of that train, wandering onto the tracks and squandering his last moments thinking, well, isn't this too bad, watching the train come at him without ever remembering he could step to the side and out of its way.

It was painful and ludicrous to recall, but he'd lost me that way at a picnic, of all places, and over a piece of chicken. He'd taken a wing to eat without finding a napkin first, and when the greasy bones lay back on his plate he looked at his fingers and then lowered his hands, palms up, under the table and out of sight with his smile wobbling because in that moment he'd forgotten he could choose between composure and humiliation. I looked away then as if something had drawn my eye, as if I hadn't been watching Byron at all, and just when I wondered how he had gotten to be an adult without knowing how to take better care of himself than that, I heard Estelle say, You look like you could use one of these. She wasn't looking at him, though, she was fixed on me with one eyebrow up to tell me I could have been the one to pass him the napkin. I should have been the one.

I stared back at her until she shook her head in irritation and reached for the iced tea jug. And even if Estelle hadn't scolded me with that look, if I'd seen only smugness and chagrin in her eyes—*You sure can pick 'em, Sappo*—nothing would have changed. Byron would still have sat there and I would have been just as unwilling to look at him or help him, if only to prevent his seeing that I was ashamed, that I was wondering what the next thing in life would be that would leave him paralyzed and impotent like that. So I went to him one evening and told him I felt we were unsuited to one other and that he shouldn't call anymore. He was too gentle to demand that I explain, or perhaps he understood that anything I could say in explanation would hurt him, and he let me go without a fight. Garfield had certainly wondered what had happened with Byron, but I had never told him a thing about it. I could never have given him the satisfaction of learning that Byron had taken the news that I no longer wanted to see him with dignity, and that his face had crumpled only in the last moment when I was leaving and he thought that I could no longer see him. And standing there with Garfield, with Byron's obit and picture on the counter in front of me, I read that he had never married, and wondered how much that had had to do with me. I had to control myself, and if Garfield was hanging around to see my reaction, why, I thought I'd give him something to see and I took the kitchen shears and cut the obit and the picture out, and then

I slid the paper back over to him and stood there until he exhaled loudly and left the room.

He was a friend, I tell Melissa, who knows somehow not to take the clipping but just looks at it on my lap. He died too young. I think she'll leave it at that, and she does. She sits back a little and breathes, Oh, and since Byron isn't the reason I'm sitting here with her, I hand her Garfield's obit. It's as brown as you like—it looks like I dipped it in tea—and it's brittle besides, but the tape has held where I stuck the pieces together. Missy holds the length of it along her palm like it's a shard of glass I've handed her. She knows as well as I do the only reason we're doing this is because we're alone, and that with Lee and Joanne both back at work and Missy here as my minder we can get up to some mischief together. I wait for her to read the thing, and then read the correction that's stuck onto the end, and when her eyes dart back up to the top and she checks and rechecks it and then looks at me in bafflement, I find I cannot look at her and look at the clipping instead.

She says, Mother told me once that Aunt Lee was with him when he died.

She what? I say, and take the clipping back, amazed, as if it were possible I'd gotten it wrong all these years, as if I could not have recited, blind, the two sentences that had left Melissa confused. But there's the one at the top: The family found that Dr. Maguire had died when they returned home from church, and then there's the correction they printed two days later, which I taped to the bottom: A report that family members found he had died after they returned home from church was in error. Dr. Maguire's daughter was with him when he died.

It had never occurred to me that Joanne would lie, and why would it? Yet there was her opportunity, right there in the correction that mentioned a daughter, but not which one. It was hardly

Joanne's fault that Porter and I had botched the correction as badly as we had the original report, and I feel myself beginning to smile at the perversity of it all. It is, after all, a sort of truth: one daughter was home with Gar that morning, and I'm tempted to forgive the lie and not expose Joanne, to understand that her seizing the occasion, conferred by chance, to lie and say it was Lee only masks a desire to confess. Still, Melissa is frowning, and so I say, I promise you, your mother was the one who was with him.

I realize now that I have only confused Melissa when what I wanted was for her to understand that everything she needs to know in order to understand her own mother is right here in this clipping. I want her to decipher the thing for herself, though, rather than be told, and that isn't going to happen just because I want it to. Not tonight. For starters, there's Joanne's lie to dislodge from Melissa's idea of what happened.

I point at the clipping and tell her, It says he was found when they returned home from church, but we didn't all go to the same church. Your mother wasn't with us. She was never with us. She was here.

I could go on and tell her what Stephen once told me, that Joanne ritually shut herself in their bedroom once a year on the anniversary of Garfield's death, or that I'd seen her myself when that anniversary fell on a weekend and she happened to be visiting, and she drove off alone to St. Paul's for most of the morning on a Saturday, looking cowed and penitent, as if she believed she deserved to be struck. I could tell Melissa that all of this changed with her birth, that Melissa herself was the thing that came the closest to pulling Joanne out of her wallowing. But more than any of those things, I could tell her that I saw Joanne's face when we came in the back door. I see it still, plain as yesterday, her eyes pleading and her mouth opening to shriek. Her voice so confused, I could hardly understand her except for one word, *Dad,*

Dad, Dad, and Lee trying to get around me until my hand stopped her and I turned her around and sent her running for the Yetters'. Lee running across our yard so fast she stumbled, running until I couldn't see her anymore, and then the crack of the Yetters' screen and Sam Yetter running toward our house.

I left Joanne by the back door then. I knew this meant that Garfield was dead and I knew where I would find him. I owed it to him to be the one to go through that last door. I owed him that much, and when I saw him a sound tore out of me that I had never heard before. I heard the kitchen door close and Sam Yetter and the girls come into the room behind me, and when I heard Lee whimper at the sight of her father there on the floor, I fell to my knees and I stayed there.

·—19—·

$\mathcal{J}$ handed the baby to Frances without thinking. There was something I had wanted to show her, something I needed both hands to pick up, so I said, Here, and I swung Joanne between us in the same motion she must once have given me Barbara Jean, and then she froze. I thought Joanne would scream. She might as well have been a live grenade the way Frances was looking at her. Porter wasn't there to catch my eye in time, to remind me that this was our changed Frances, the Frances who didn't hold babies, who didn't want reminding. She stood there in shock, and I thought for sure Joanne would start to cry because no one had ever looked at her like something was wrong. Like she was the thing that was wrong.

I was used to giving the baby to Estelle, who took her each time as if she'd just been given the biggest present from under the tree. It was often hard to get her to surrender Joanne when it was time to leave, so hard she'd usually press her cheek against Joanne's, say, Nope, and walk away from me, but with Frances I'd half expected her to fling the baby back at me like we were playing Hot Potato. Joanne was evidently too stunned to cry, and the two of them eyed each other anxiously until Frances exhaled and settled Joanne on her hip, and Joanne began to pull at Frances's brooch.

Losing Barbara Jean had taken some of the loveliness from

Frances's face. She had been lovely before in a gentle way that you saw if you truly looked at her, or when Porter came into the room and that softness and the secret almost-smile entered her eyes. She was older now—it was nine years since Barbara Jean had lived and died—but it seemed to me that Frances's blurring jawline and the austerity of her chignon had less to do with time than with grief.

Frances had never had any particular ambitions of her own beyond high school and when it became clear she would not have a family of her own, she settled into keeping a home for Porter. In some ways it felt as if Barbara Jean had never happened. As if they had married and begun an uninterrupted cycle of breakfasts and dinners and work and Sunday roasts in their modest and immaculate home. There wasn't anything to remind you that there had been that interruption, that for a short while there had been a frenzy of knitting and preparation and then for six months there had been diapers to boil and a cradle and toys and even photographs of the baby. All of that was simply gone and they hadn't asked for any help in removing any of it. Everything was gone and we didn't ask whether it was saved or given away. Whether the photos were in a box or a drawer and might come out again with time, whether there might even be another child one day to fit into that cradle and those clothes. I knew and Estelle knew, too, that they had separate beds from that point. Still in the same room and with one table between them for a nightstand, but the old bed had gone, and none of us knew where. There never was another baby, and we were all as silent as if they had simply always been barren.

Years on, when we all picnicked together in a park one Saturday afternoon, I told them I wanted a snapshot before we left, and they sat, high and low, on the near side of the picnic table for me. I couldn't get everyone to look at the camera at the same time—

they were all content and full, looking this way and that and still talking—so I gave up trying and took the picture anyway. I never showed it to anyone once it was developed. I looked at it long and hard myself, before I put it at the bottom of a shoebox with other photos. There were a few other photos from that day to put in the album, and when no one asked after it and no one remembered, I decided I didn't need to be the one to remind them.

Only Garfield and Lillian had managed to look at the camera. It's the first picture of all of us taken after the war, and one of the very last photos we had of Lillian. She's got her hands crossed over her pocketbook in her lap and her hair done up like it's 1910. She's sitting primly, knees and ankles together, still a big-boned woman, but her spine is slumped and no longer up to the task. She looks in danger of puddling into her own lap, done in by the weight of the cameo at the neck of her dress. She and Garfield are both squinting at the camera—there never was any use in waiting for either of them to smile—and Garfield had made a mess of his tie that morning and left the back of it hanging three inches longer than the front. Joanne is slumped too, next to Lillian, but it's just the little girl sag of someone who is daydreaming and who still hasn't been told to sit up straight enough years in a row that it happens automatically.

Porter is holding Lee, who is all of four months. She's got her fist in her mouth, waiting for a feeding, and she's leaning against Porter like he's a recliner. You'd never believe that she isn't his own child, the ease with which they lean into each other, unguarded and entirely themselves. Porter is curled around her, his knees pressed together to make a better lap, and he holds her heels lightly in his palms, like they're tiny balls of yarn that he just might decide to start juggling at any moment. I can't picture Garfield holding a child, any child, like this. He'd have his hands under Lee's arms, ready to hoist her. He'd give her one leg at most to sit on, and tell anyone who asked that she was already learning to balance.

Estelle is on Porter's other side, at the end of the bench. She's staring off in the same direction as Joanne, so lost suddenly you'd think she didn't know the rest of us were there. She was a war widow then, still between Jack and Walter, and when her eyes veered off at something no one else could see, we tended to leave her alone. My saying that I wanted a family photo likely put her in mind of Jack, but even reminded of his absence and suddenly melancholy, she's still beautiful, she's the one who draws your eye. That is, until you see Frances.

Another person would only think that she'd been caught mid-expression, that the shutter had closed just as she was beginning to look up, just beginning to smile. But her smile is leaving, it's sliding off her face and she's powerless to stop herself from looking at Porter in that moment when no one is looking at her, when I'm laughing and telling everyone for the third time, *Say cheese!* Because Porter is there in front of her, holding a four-month-old child.

I put that photo out of my mind once I'd laid it in the shoebox. I forgot it so completely that when Porter came looking for photos, years later, not long after Frances had died, I put the shoebox out with a stack of photo albums on the table in front of him and I went out to the kitchen to make us some coffee. He'd only wanted any photos he didn't have copies of himself, and I told him he could take any of them he liked, but when I came back, I found him with that picnic table photo in his hand, as if he'd known all along that it was there, waiting at the bottom of that box. He wiped his eyes over and over, and said, She told me she didn't want to try again, and I believed her.

I'd seen it, too, I wanted to tell him, more than twenty years ago, and if I didn't say anything then it was because I had believed they'd decided against more children, that they shouldn't have them, or couldn't, since Frances was past forty when the picture was taken. I put our coffee cups on the table and sat down next to Porter. Frances was already dead. Would it do anything more than break his heart again if I told him? And when he glanced at me and laughed and said, Look at the two of us, I realized I was crying, and I found my handkerchief and pressed my eyes hard because I understood now why they had waited to tell me that my mother had died, and that what I had done to Porter was no different.

When I picture Frances now, I see it all in reverse. Her face, the afternoon I forgot myself and handed her a baby. Her face, the day we buried Barbara Jean, who died of a bowel obstruction at the age of six months. Her face, when Barbara Jean had been born and I tiptoed in to see them asleep together in the wide bed.

20

*W*here was Mount Cenis, Garfield wanted to know. It was Porter who was meant to answer; the rest of us were there to listen. There weren't many people who were willing to spar with Garfield, not many who were able, but Garfield had found out somehow that Porter enjoyed geography, and that he had developed a pretty fair memory for odd places as well as his schoolboy's store of capitals and kingdoms. I should have seen that Garfield would turn it into a contest, that he would never be content with good-natured conversation, but none of us saw it, perhaps not even Garfield, himself. They didn't have a great deal in common, those two, and testing each other on points of geography seemed, in the beginning, to be a boon, and no more precarious than their deciding to arm wrestle for the last cigarette in the pack.

It was in the Alps, Porter said, and Garfield grinned and nodded. Yes, it certainly was. Perhaps that had been too easy. Did Porter know anything notable about it? He did. Indeed, he did. It had been an important mountain pass between France and Italy for centuries. Used by pilgrims, if he wasn't mistaken, on their way to Rome. Very good, very good. Garfield nodded appreciatively. It had even been used militarily by Charlemagne and Hannibal, although Hannibal was disputed. My, my, Garfield laughed. He'd have to get up earlier if he was ever going to stump Porter.

Lee came running then with a fistful of purple clover for Frances, who put the flowers in an empty drinking glass in the middle of the picnic table. She sent Lee off again with the first brownie off the plate, set the thermos of coffee out, and told us to help ourselves. I was full and feeling drowsy, lulled by the food and the afternoon light that was golden and clear. Frances and I had scraped the plates into a paper sack and stacked them, spread tea towels over the potato salad bowl and what remained of the chicken, and I'd sat down again and lit a cigarette. It was Saturday, and there was nothing any of us needed to do but sit in the park. There was nothing that wanted doing once we got home, either. The picnic had been Porter and Frances's idea, and all the dishes and leftovers would go home with them in their car. I'd even done the ironing for Sunday church before we left the house.

Joanne was lying on a blanket, reading. She was still wearing the dandelion bracelet Lee had made for her, so absorbed by her book she'd forgotten it. I watched her, propped up on her elbows and turning the pages so often another person might have thought she was skimming her book. Lee was collecting more flowers, and I thought about telling her to stop. They'd just wither without water, and we could hardly put them in coffee. But then there was nothing else for her to do, no slide or swings nearby, and the river here looked about the same as it looked at home, fifteen miles north.

It was Porter's turn. What were the Pillars of Hercules, he wanted to know, and made Garfield laugh. Why, they were promontories at the Strait of Gibraltar. Even Lee likely knew that much. Fine, and what are they called? Garfield waved Lee over. Couldn't she tell Uncle Porter what she thought of when she heard the word Gibraltar? Rock, she said. The Rock of Gibraltar. Fine, fine, and the other one? Well, now, Garfield needed to think. Wasn't that a point of dispute, like Hannibal? Yes, it certainly was. Either of the disputed promontories would be acceptable. Garfield needed some coffee. He wasn't sure; he thought he'd seen it not long ago somewhere. He'd recognize it the moment he heard it. Did Garfield give up? Well, he supposed he did, although if the point was in dispute, you might say that he'd given a complete answer already. Jebel Musa. Yes, of course, Jebel Musa. How interesting.

Porter had rolled up his shirtsleeves and lit a cigarette. He thought the game was over. The sun had gone down behind the trees and he could push his straw hat a little further back on his head. He could have a brownie and some coffee from the thermos, could someone pass them, please? How was he at islands, Garfield wanted to know. Mountains, islands; Porter couldn't say he preferred one over the other. What about the Gilbert and Ellice Islands? They were in the Pacific. And? They were British. And? Porter thought they were part of an atoll. And the capital? Porter didn't know. Tarawa was the capital, Garfield said. Well, now, how about that. Porter drank some coffee and lit another cigarette. Did Garfield know anything about Brusnik Island, he wanted to know. Garfield was surprised, he thought they would have left the Pacific. Brusnik Island lay off the coast of New Zealand. Porter shook his head, flicked his ash onto a saucer. No? Did the rules of the game allow for Garfield to have a think and stretch his legs? They did.

Gar sauntered off to a stand of trees, but then walked back double-time. The Adriatic. Porter nodded and gave a cold sort of smile. He held the pack of cigarettes out to Garfield. Surely the game was over. Garfield squinted at Porter over the smoke from the cigarette he had lit and left to dangle from his lips. He poured more coffee for them both. I caught Frances's eye. When had either of us last seen Porter angry? Had we ever? Joanne turned her pages. Lee found flowers, bent their stems and snapped them.

Garfield was smirking now. We'd love this next one, his eyes seemed to say. The one where he held his foot over Porter's throat and we all took bets on how long he would keep it there. I got up from the table, but purposely trod on my own toe so that I would stumble. My coffee was only warm by then, it wouldn't have burned him, but Gar hollered with surprise all the same when it hit the back of his shirt. The shirt was likely ruined now, and Garfield was up from the table and looking at me as if I had lost my mind. Over his shoulder, I saw the flicker of a smile on Porter's face before we both had to look away from each other.

I turned Garfield back around and started blotting his shirt with the tea towel Frances had handed me. She, Porter, and I were all working hard not to meet each other's eye, all of us too well bred to laugh out loud, although laughing at Garfield Maguire—the three of us together—might well have been enough to stop him.

The Islets of Langerhans, Garfield said, and Porter's face fell. He stared sorrowfully at Gar. He poured his coffee out onto the grass. He got up and Frances got up with him. They began to pack the dishes. Porter didn't know. He didn't suppose anyone did, and Garfield had surely won this time. He and Frances should be heading home. Lee and Joanne both stopped what they were doing and watched. I took the cup out of Garfield's hand, poured his coffee out and helped pack. Porter and Frances kissed the girls. Frances got in the car. Didn't he want to hear the answer, Garfield wanted to know. Porter stopped with his hand on the door handle, his knuckles showing white, his jaw tight. All right. Where were the Islets of Langerhans.

Why, they were in the pancreas, of course. Garfield howled, and Porter gave him a slow, wry smile, got in the car, and drove away. Garfield held out his hands, palms up, and watched them recede.

When had everyone lost their sense of humor, he wanted to know. He turned to look at me. Couldn't a fellow have any fun?

21

*N*o one was surprised when Estelle looked like a film star in her senior portrait. She had even thought to buy a length of netting to wear like a shawl. It was the black sort that was meant for widows, but Estelle had crumpled it and floated it around her shoulders, knowing somehow that it would soften her dark dress, and that against the diffuse background in the photographer's studio, she would look as if she were emerging from a sepia haze. She wore no makeup—our father never allowed it—but it wouldn't have improved a thing if she had. Mother had convinced him to let her get a marcel, though, and she'd pinned her hair up at the neck to look as if it were bobbed. She doesn't look full of herself—it would have been intolerable if her gaze had been haughty or vain—her face is open, straightforward; she is wearing the beginnings of a smile at the corners of her eyes and mouth. I've heard people say since that you're supposed to look at the camera as if you're in love with it, but Estelle did them one better, and all at the age of eighteen, with eyes that say *I might just be in love with you.*

Years on, Estelle surprised me greatly by accepting old age with grace. She blended in more and more with the crowd and never once complained. But she only blended; she didn't fade. Estelle remained a clothes horse to the end, having outlived three husbands and several dogs, she was the old lady with the good handbag and fresh lipstick in her pew of a Sunday morning. And if her Mona Lisa smile made you wonder whether she was hankering after the past, she was. Not to go back and stay, but to do it all again, every bit of it, and still find herself white-haired and thick in the middle, sitting at the end of that pew. And if she didn't cry in the church or at the cemetery after Harry died, it was likely because she'd fully expected to be left alone a third time. That whole week with Estelle felt as if our visit had been planned months in advance, not patched together in haste and with expense after a late-night phone call. Harry's reading glasses and ashtray were tidied away before we arrived, and Estelle had already taken to sitting in his chair, to prevent its becoming a melancholy object. She fooled us all. She'd been widowed before, and her tidy house, her full refrigerator, the sandwiches she made us every day at noon, the dry-eyed grace she said each night at supper, all seemed to say that she was fine. She was already fine and there was nothing for us to wait around or to hope for, but when we were at the airport, she cried and couldn't stop when she had to say good-bye to Melissa, and it seemed that Estelle had mostly fooled herself, and Melissa, who was all of eleven, stood there promising to come back soon because the plane was boarding and Estelle was sputtering and refusing to let go of her arm.

Estelle would have surprised Garfield, if he could have lived to see that he'd been wrong about her, about the curse of beauty. Estelle had been beautiful, but she'd come out all right. And Estelle's not gone, not really. How can she be when she looks out at me from Lee's face, when Lee even moves like Estelle did, as if her hips should have been just a half an inch further apart. I miss her as I never believed I would, and no one has called me Sappo in the years since she died, but then no one else ever did. We did Estelle a disservice, thinking she was less substantial than she was, believing that a woman who was widowed, divorced, and childless could never be happy. It's true that, if you look at a photo of me holding Joanne and then at another where Estelle's got her, it's clear which sister is the mother and which is the aunt. Estelle doesn't look tired, for one, but more than that, it's the way she's smiling like a child of ten who has just been given a puppy. Whenever Estelle held one of my babies, I watched her. Sometimes, early on, she wondered if she'd had the baby for too long and tried to hand her back, but I'd shake my head and smile, not because I was tired and wanted a break, but because I was busy watching Estelle.

Porter held my babies as a father would, as someone who was still a father would. But Estelle looked for all the world as if we'd been holding out on her, as if she'd been the last to hear how it felt to hold a baby who shared blood with you, and weren't the rest of us a bunch of dopes for being so composed. She never surprised me more than she did then, when she held Joanne so I could take a picture and their blond heads were white in the sun, and Estelle pressed her cheek to Joanne's, both of them elated and radiant. My sister and my child. *How wonderful! We never knew.*

And then came all the years, the decades, when I hardly saw her, when she'd married Harry and they'd moved to Denver and bought a gas station and sent a wall calendar each year with a picture of it and the words *Lynch's Garage* in black letters across the top. We got out there a couple of times to visit them, and they came home to visit us, and I didn't worry about her. By the time I was old enough to realize I could worry about my older sister, that I was supposed to worry about her even though she was older, there was nothing to worry about. We took turns phoning each other and she'd say, What's new, Sappo, which made me laugh because how much could be new each week on Sunday.

Standing in the cemetery in Denver, waiting for Estelle to go into the ground next to Harry, I was suddenly the only one left who remembered it all. How wide open Estelle's eyes always were when we were children, how she never seemed to blink. How Porter hunched over when he sat, because he was taller, so much longer than everyone else. How we each tried to be first to holler that Dad was home when we heard his footfalls on the walk. How Mother brushed Dad's hand away from her hip because she'd grown so round, and how she smiled when he put his hand right back again. And what they all would have remembered of me, I have no idea. They were all of them in the ground.

I stood there, sputtering and wobbling, with Joanne and Lee, all of us in black and hiding behind our shades, truly uncertain whether I should laugh or cry because I finally understood that Estelle had loved my girls in part and perhaps mostly because they were mine. And I ended up smiling because I remembered Harry and Estelle at my kitchen table, white-haired and stout, and Estelle teasing him, calling him Old Man, and taking both of Harry's hands, the real one and the wooden one too, because Estelle had been beautiful once and knew that that white glove and its wooden hand were not Harry, that neither his hands nor his scars made him Harry.

And Harry smiled at her and said, I've still got you, don't I? I've still got you.

·—22—·

*J*oanne is breathtaking; she is transfigured. It's one thing to know that a person is full of anger, and it's an easy thing to point and say, that person over there, the one who is functioning and is to all appearances calm, is really just a cauldron of rage, but it's something else entirely to see the whole snarled mess coming apart in front of you, and if Joanne has finally achieved a fit she can't control, it might as well be because of me and it might as well be happening in my kitchen.

I've got a hand on Lee's arm to keep her silent and in her chair, but I can't do anything about her face. She'd cheerfully take Joanne's throat in her hands right now, just to feel what forty odd years of anger felt like, coming out all at once. I wish I could stop Joanne long enough to reassure Lee and Missy, to tell them to hunker down and let Joanne blow. She can't hurt us. She's raging about things, about objects, not even people. It's riveting, really, seeing her like this. I wonder that the expression on my face alone hasn't been enough to stop her because I'm not looking at her, I'm observing, watching a display. Joanne in flames, burning herself out.

What else have you given her? Joanne shouts, and, heaven help her, she glances down at my left hand to see if I'm still wearing my wedding ring.

145

I hold a hand up to stop Lee from answering for me and say, Any gift I give Melissa is between Melissa and me.

If you give her a family heirloom, it's my business. Don't I count? Doesn't Lee count?

Again, I have to silence Lee. She can't see that this has nothing to do with her or Melissa. It has nothing to do with me, for that matter. I could say that all of this had put me in mind of nothing so much as waiting for a toddler to exhaust herself with thrashing and wailing on the floor, but Joanne would take that as mockery. A spur to her fury.

Should I give everything to you first, so you can decide?

Yes, if you're going to be irresponsible!

Was it irresponsible to give Missy my onyx ring? Did you want it?

What else did you give her? She's shrieking and I'd like to get Bill on the phone, but he wouldn't be any use. He shams his way through Joanne's moods, just rolls up like a pill bug and pretends it isn't happening. And now Melissa is in tears. She's not even looking at anyone. She's got her hands together on the table, and it might look like she's hiding the onyx ring, but she's not. She's got ahold of it like she's ready to rip it off, and if she does I hope she flings it across the room. I don't even think Melissa likes the ring that much. She's wearing it to be polite. Look where that got her.

Damma— Missy says, and I shake my head.

You don't have to listen to this, Missy, you don't even have to be here, I tell her, but then Joanne starts around the table like she's headed for the back bedroom to go through Missy's things.

My wedding dress, I say to stop Joanne. I gave her my wedding dress. She turns to look at me, and I can see she's not done yet, so I say, You remember, the one I offered to you when you got married that you weren't interested in?

What else.

I'm surprised that she can see me that clearly right now, that she can see I'm still holding back.

Mother's crystal necklace, I tell her. I like saying that as little as she likes hearing it, and her eyes are as injured as if Melissa were, right now, wearing the dress and the necklace in front of her, the necklace Joanne covets and was once brazen enough to ask me for outright.

I gave it to her because it gave me pleasure, I want to scream. Because it was mine to give and it gave me pleasure to put it into Melissa's hands when my wedding dress was already lying across her lap. Something of mine, and something of my mother's, in the same moment. Because the first thing Melissa did once I'd handed it to her was not to put it on and preen, but to look behind her at the portrait of my mother on the table by the hall door instead, and she was right: Mother is wearing the necklace in that photo, and even I'd forgotten. Because I was there when Dad gave the necklace to Mother and I saw both of their faces when she opened the box. Mother, astonished that Dad had somehow divined the very necklace she'd loved and thought too dear, and Dad, trying hard not to laugh when what he wanted to say was, Emma, sweetheart, a blind man could have seen how badly you wanted that necklace, because he'd known when they walked past the jeweler's window that the thing she allowed her eyes to flick across just once was the thing she thought most fine. Because if I'd given the necklace to Lee it would only have been to spite Joanne and her entitlement, and because Missy should have something from me, directly from me, without her mother deciding when exactly she can have it.

I want to tell Joanne that she should be ashamed. That her own child could not accept the simple gifts of a string of crystal beads and a wedding dress so old the stitching was gone in places without worry. That she'd given me an uneasy smile and said,

Mother's not going to like your giving all of this away, and would only finally laugh when I'd made a face and said we'd tell Joanne I was joining a convent. I want to ask Joanne what she imagines I felt when Melissa tried the dress and necklace on together, whether she thinks it weighs on me at all to know that I likely won't live to see Melissa married. How it feels right now to know that Melissa's worry wasn't in the least misplaced, and that my own daughter evidently values things more than she values us.

All of this will go to Melissa eventually, I say instead. I'm just speeding the process up. I say this as if it's a considered policy I've decided upon. It used to be fun, outmaneuvering Joanne. Telling her, yes, you can cut the cake, but then Lee gets to choose which piece she wants. I'd have thought we'd be done with this nonsense by now. It's tiring, always having to be the slyer fox.

It's not that Joanne is averse to change. Change itself is fine, as long as it's Joanne who's changing things. I'd like a nickel for every time she's stomped through my living room, bellyaching, I wish to God there was a phone jack in the kitchen. There's not enough light in this hall. And then I'd like a dollar for every tradesman she would hire to modernize the place, for each all-important change. Phone jacks in at least three rooms. My ancient fridge gone, and some glossy, silent monster in its place. A tumble dryer in favor of my drying lines in the basement, although I think she'd keep the line outside between the garage and the mulberry tree for the charm of it, for the picture of a white bed sheet, flapping on a summer day. My kitchen and bathroom carpeting are unhygienic—I know, because she told me. She'd get tile in, something neutral, tasteful, and she'd swap my bathtub for a shower cabinet besides.

And the only thing Joanne likes less than not being in control is having her lack of control pointed out for her. I saw it first when she was a baby, not yet six months old, when I'd put her on a blanket on the floor in Lillian's living room so she could look out the front window. We'd been out visiting someone or other that day, and I was tired. I put Joanne down so I could start our supper, and thought she'd be fine there a little while on her own. I could hear her babbling and drumming her heels on the floor, and when it became clear she was working herself into a froth and her babbling turned to wailing, I thought she was just overtired, but when I went in and saw what she was looking at, my mouth fell right open. It was a still summer day, and Joanne, red with fury, could not fathom why the tattoo of her heels had not made the branches or the leaves on Lillian's oak tree dance. This was priceless, Garfield and Lillian said when I told them at dinner, and proof of high intelligence. Why shouldn't the oak boughs dance, when Joanne's mobile did her bidding if she drummed her heels in her crib? It foreboded brilliance, they said, and what ever was that look on my face meant to be?

I'd been warned, you might say, from nearly the beginning, and by Joanne herself. Still, I'm unprepared when she slaps a legal pad on the table and marks the top page off in columns. I wonder first if she imagines we're all going to be pals now and play Yahtzee or Rummy, but she's got their three names at the tops of the columns and not mine.

Who's getting what, she wants to know.

My eyes flash warning, but she can't see that. I wonder that she can even see to write, whipped up as she is.

I drew up a will for that, I say.

Good, she says. Then it won't be hard to remember. She's ready to write and looking so wounded you'd think she'd heard I was giving everything to the neighbor's cat. You've already parted with Grandma's crystal necklace, how about Gran Maguire's crystal goblets?

Lee smiles an unholy smile then, and I wince. I can't stop her and I won't even try. She leans toward Joanne, gripping the edge of the table. They're gone, she says. If Joanne were to slap her right now, I don't think Lee would even feel it.

I lay my hand on Lee's arm. Don't say anything you'll regret, I tell her, and she explodes.

Don't say anything *I'll* regret? Tell her that!

What do you mean they're gone?

They went in the garage sale, which you'd know if you'd bothered to help, Lee says.

Joanne pushes back from the table. She goes to the sink and I think she's looking for something to smash but she holds onto the counter instead, and she holds on so hard I believe she could rip a chunk of it right out if she wanted to. She says, My grandmother drank out of those glasses. My father drank out of those glasses.

I stop listening then. I'm overwhelmed suddenly and trying not to hear, but Lee is reminding Joanne that Lillian was also her grandmother and Garfield was her father, and Joanne is yelling that she didn't even know the one and could hardly remember the other, and I could tell them both that I remembered them well enough for everyone and that if I let the glasses go in a garage sale it was because I thought there were enough other things to leave my daughters and because they didn't matter to me.

What about my *Little Lulu*s? Lee is yelling now.

Your what?

My comic books. The ones you gave to that collector friend of yours.

Joanne looks at the ceiling and breathes out slowly, letting Lee see how tiresome it is to have to answer her. Since you were an adult by then, she says, I had thought that you were done with them.

Melissa wasn't.

What?

Melissa! She read them every time she was here. She used to go straight down to the basement and bring up the whole stack and sit and read them.

I don't remember that.

How can you not remember that? She sat in the chair with the ottoman and read them over and over again. And before you say it didn't matter, that she had her own comic books, let me remind you that they were not yours to give away but you did it anyway.

Are you actually suggesting that your comic books have the same value as family heirlooms?

I can't stand it anymore and I say in a voice so low it is almost menacing, Stop it now. Both of you. They look at me, each of them, as if I've just taken the other's side, baffled that I'm about to let such obvious injustice go unchecked.

I did not become a mother to see this, I say. I did not raise either of you to behave like this. They're both crying now, and just as predictably as if they were actors performing a script, Lee slumps where she's standing like someone's let the air out of her, and Joanne pushes past us, sputtering her way into the living room. I get up from the table to go after her. There's nothing I can say to Melissa now, so I put my hand on her shoulder as I go out, and when I sit next to Joanne on the davenport, I reach my arms around her and I wonder when the last time I did this was. She leans right into me, suddenly a child, my child, and I wonder if I have a clean hankie in my pocket I can give her and I stroke her hair because she's letting me and I tell her, I'm not going anywhere just yet.

·—23—·

*T*he baby was sick. I rocked her, gave her my breast, but she refused. Curled her head away, back into my palm, and bellowed under my nipple. The mantel clock struck two. Garfield walked the floor, scowling at his feet.

Can't you rub her gums with whiskey the way you did Joanne's, he said.

This isn't teething, Gar, and it isn't a fit. She's hot. I don't know what I can give her.

Garfield saw the door ajar. Come in, Joanne, he said.

I closed my nightgown when Joanne pushed open the door and came to me to look at the baby. Garfield stopped her. Stay away.

What's wrong with Lee? Joanne asked.

She has a fever and it's making her cry, I said. Garfield, please call Dr. Gower.

I'll call him in the morning, he said. I won't wake a man at two a.m. for a fever. Imagine if I ran across town for every midnight toothache.

Feel her, Gar. She's so hot and she's coughing. I never saw Joanne like this.

Margaret, he said, frowning and holding a finger to his lips. Back to bed, Joanne. I'll tuck you in again.

But I want to hold her, Joanne said. She never cries when I hold her.

That's because she's never crying when we give her to you. Garfield steered Joanne into the hall with a hand on the top of her head. They were both shouting as they left the room.

I still want to try.

No, he said. We don't want two sick children.

Once they were gone, Lee's squalling crowded in on me so. Cool water, I thought. Strip the baby naked and wash her, pour water over her and milk the fever out.

I laid her on the counter on a folded towel and pushed soft rags underneath the water I had trapped in the kitchen sink. With my hand wet, I stroked her, and then with the dripping rags, I covered her. I laid the rags in strips across each leg, her shuddering belly, her arms. I rubbed her brow once more with wet fingers before I covered it, to wash away the redness and the sweat, but the water hurried from her head and the oily sweat remained. I wrapped her head and laid the last rag across her throat. Lee fretted against the sodden cloth. She began to look like a specimen to me, a tiny wild thing plastered to a board. I weighed down the rags with water that I carried with my fingers closed like a spoon, and her kicking stopped. She still trembled, shaken by unseen hands, but her eyes were closed. Silence rang in my ears.

THE DOCTOR told us it was a cold, told us *keep her warm and make a poultice*, and I rubbed her with goose fat and garlic and wrapped her in flannel. But days passed, and then a week, and when the doctor returned because the baby was worse, he said, *whooping cough*, and *no one could have known*.

Her coughing became hideous. I waited through the fits, holding her upright while she coughed and her face turned red and then black and blue, as if she were bruised. I waited for the whoop, the reverberating gasp that ended one fit and began the next.

When the spasms ended, she spat up viscid sputum that I collected in a metal basin that I held under her chin. I wiped her face with a damp rag, and I showed the basin to Garfield, unsure of what to do next. Let it collect, he said. I'll burn it tonight.

Garfield wound a wide cloth around Lee's middle, wrapped it tight so that she would not herniate in spasm. We held our breath for the minute each spasm took, watching the successive coughs drive air from the baby's lungs, so that her head seemed to swell and her eyes to protrude before the fit vanished in a whoop. We looked at each other once she was quiet in exhausted, painful relief, but soon even that grew hard, just seeing each other like that was too hard, and we stopped. After that, it felt like we were enduring it all separately, as if we each had a baby, both in equal danger, both equally sick.

At night, when the fits were longer and worse, I rocked Lee in the living room by the picture window with its curtains open and the shadow of the pear tree cast in by the post lamp. Between the fits, when she lay trembling on my chest, I slept.

Joanne found me sitting there one night. I woke when I heard her feet on the carpet but kept my eyes closed and my head tilted back against the headrest of the rocker. She touched my arm and then took her hand away. I kept my eyes closed, but she did it again, and I knew that I would see her face full of pleading when I finally did look. Pleading the way she had the time I told her she was too big to carry and she said, I'll jump up. You only have to catch me.

I looked at her finally and whispered, You can't keep getting out of bed like this.

Joanne stood there, her nightgown pale and her hair luminous in the light from the post lamp. I can't sleep when she coughs, she said.

I imagine not. But you can try to sleep in between the coughs like your dad and I do, can't you?

Why were you smiling? Is the baby better now?

Was I smiling? I suppose I was dreaming. You're a good girl to worry. I brushed her hand away from the baby's back. Don't, I said. You might wake her and get her coughing again.

Is she always going to be sick? We shouldn't keep her if she's always going to be sick.

Ye gad, Joanne! What a thing to say. We certainly aren't giving her away. We need to pray for her.

How?

The same as always. You just ask God to keep the baby from danger.

Joanne laid her hand on the armrest, where the finish had rubbed away and the wood was soft and tacky if you rubbed it. Her hand moved with the rocker, in and out of shadow, and she watched the baby.

I can't smell you anymore, she said.

Whatever do you mean?

I only smell the baby.

That's the poultice.

She stood there, very still, except for her hand on the arm of the rocker, and frowned.

What is it, Joanne?

What about the girl who died?

What girl who died? Do you mean Ruth? I wanted to jump up then and fling the photo of Gar and his sisters at him in his sleep. Lillian had shown that picture to Joanne one too many times, telling her she was the image of her little Ruth who'd died of scarlet fever at the age of five. Joanne asked to see the photo so often after that that Gar finally framed it and left it out for her on a shelf. Ruth was scowling in the picture, as if she'd known what was coming, and Lillian had never been able to look at the photo without shaking her head and saying, Ruth always did belong more to God.

Joanne whispered, What if God wants this baby with him, too?

Joanne, you act as if you don't want to pray for her! I hissed. We must all pray that she comes through this. Now go back to bed, or you'll wake her for certain.

Lee stirred once when Joanne had gone. Her fist fluttered on my chest. I watched her head and listened to her breath, to the wheeze and bubble, waiting for the one that would catch in her throat and send her into spasm. I closed my eyes with my hand still on her back, tried to quiet my breathing, and I waited.

Garfield carried the metal basin of sputum outside each night. I would watch him when I could, as he stood near the burn can and splashed the inside of the basin with alcohol before he struck a match against the brick wall of the garage. He waited for the blaze to diminish, for the match to begin to consume itself, before he let it fall from his fingertips into the basin. He set the basin in the gravel then, until the alcohol had burned itself out and only charred sludge remained, and then he flushed it with water from an old can and slid the mess into the hole he had dug for the purpose beside the driveway.

Yellow light would fall from the kitchen windows in rectangles onto the gravel, and Garfield would sit on one of the timber posts along the driveway watching his basin burn, while I sat on the kitchen stoop watching Gar. As long as it was quiet, we would both remain outdoors. I knew Joanne was watching, too, each night from her dark window. If Gar knew she was there, he never said so. We'd both watch him sitting there, or pacing, or leaning his head back to search through the pine canopy for stars. He caught Joanne one day, digging in those holes. Caught her poking at one of them with a stick and grabbed her by the sleeve and spanked her hard, shouting, *Never, never, never!* So she started to play in the front yard after that, and dug her own holes to bury the rotted pears and crabapples she found there in the grass.

Joanne watched everything from windows and doorways then. She'd stare at our backs from the hall when we were bent over Lee's crib, or when we sat exhausted in the straight-backed chair beside the crib in turns to watch the baby and our heads drooped the way sunflowers' heavy faces fold down upon their stalks. She stood in places we couldn't see her, where we couldn't tell her to go back to bed or go outside. She made no noise. I came upon her one day when she'd come home from school and hadn't said a word. I found her sitting at the kitchen table with her coat still on, eating bread and butter, and was as shocked by the sight of her as if she'd been a raccoon come in to forage.

After a month had passed, the baby began to run in my dreams. She chased Joanne, and grew, only swollen at first, then inflating enormously like a hot-air balloon. Joanne ran, too, trying to escape, but the baby followed her and, as she grew, her skin became thin as a membrane, snagging on the black, dead trees, threatening to burst. There were tree roots Joanne couldn't see, pushing up like jutting elbows through the ground to snatch at her feet. She couldn't get up again once she fell, but crawled away backward, scuttling on her palms and the soles of her feet, the baby's face still there above her, leering black and blue, bobbing where it was caught among the branches.

I woke to the sound of my own yelling, or maybe it was the baby's coughing that woke me, but I heard her in any case and I went in to Gar to take her for a while and let him sleep. I was parched inside. I had felt more so with each passing week, and no less so because of Garfield, who had begun to wear a look of futility, as if our taking turns to sit up all night every night with the baby was of little use, as if it would end in our losing her all the same.

We had waited years for the next baby after Joanne, who had come so easily, so soon. Six years before the second one, and that ended in the toilet. My mouth curled at the bitter thought of it: my soiled nightgown and the red bloom in the water. And after seven years, this baby. Lee. It was a long wait, Margaret, Garfield had said when he took her to hold for the first time. But seven is a holy number, even for Presbyterians.

When I came into the room, Garfield couldn't hear me over the baby's crying, but he turned when he realized I was there and I thought my knees would give out from under me. Lee's face was different. Dark blood hung in ropes from her nose and mouth, dripping into the basin Gar held beneath her chin.

Oh, my God! I shouted with my hands over my mouth. Oh, Jesus, no!

Margaret, Margaret, Garfield was crying. I had never seen him cry. The doctor said this might happen. It's the strain of the cough, it's only the strain.

I wiped her face with a cloth and it smeared the blood across her lips and chin. The whoop came then, and she vomited into the basin, sputtering and shaking in Garfield's arms. I sobbed into my hands, She's only a baby, she's only a baby.

Maybe the baby's dying, said Joanne from the doorway. Neither Gar nor I had seen her there. She was only seven, she couldn't have heard the unspoken wish in her own voice.

I tried to speak first, to say what I had been saying all along, that the baby wasn't dying, that she'd turn the corner soon, but there was Garfield, with his terrible eyes and his hand flung out, pointing at Joanne.

Never say that again! You brought this home with you from school, you made her sick! You make me ashamed. Ashamed!

Joanne recoiled into the dark hallway. I never saw her face. She ran back to her room, and when I turned around again, Gar had started for the kitchen. He stood, shaking, at the kitchen sink with Lee on his hip, wetting and wringing out a washcloth to clean her face. I had no words when I looked at him, I waited until he looked away from Lee long enough to see my bewildered and angry face. I let him see that I was not simply silent, but that I was literally speechless with fury, before I went to find Joanne in her room.

She was in her bed, with her back to the door. I lay down with her, but when I touched her shoulder, she pulled away. There was nothing I could say, no trick I could use to ease her out of shock and into plain crying. If I'd said he didn't mean it, we'd both have known that I was lying. I lay my hand on her hair, but she pulled away again, jerking more emphatically toward the edge of the bed, until she lay right up against the wall.

I stayed there with her until I knew she was asleep. I could never have explained to her then that I was the one who had failed her, that I had agreed by my silence that she was Garfield's to raise and not mine. I had failed her, and that was the reason why, when Garfield had held Lee in his arms that very first time, I had taken her back and said, This one is mine.

— 24 —

J thought more and more that Garfield had always wished he'd learned to play the piano himself. There was no other reason for his always sitting there in his chair when one of the girls practiced or when I played. Always with his ankles crossed on the ottoman and a *Britannica* open on his lap, his hands resting on the pages, not reading, just letting his head fall back against the chair with his eyes closed and his glasses pulled so low the bows were just balanced on the tops of his ears. He always had the *Britannica*, always had the lamp switched on to create the impression that he had only sat down to read, and he generally did read once the practicing was over and the music put away, and sometimes he stayed there so long he fell asleep in the lamplight and only came to bed when I had already been asleep for hours. He wasn't sitting there for the pleasure of the music, though. He was loitering. A cat feigning sleep outside the mouse's hole.

Joanne was long past needing my help on the piano, and I took to sitting in the kitchen with a cup of coffee and the evening paper while she played, telling myself that if I left her alone to practice, she'd know that I trusted her, that I recognized how accomplished she had become. I had time out there to think in the spaces between her playing and Garfield's commenting, and I suspected more and more that Gar was jealous, even as I told myself it was preposterous, his being jealous of talent that had come largely, maybe even mostly, from him. But there was no other explanation for the way he built her up and tore her down, and if she played soullessly, joylessly, it was only because she'd learned that precision and technical perfection would keep him silent.

He couldn't play the piano and I had never once heard him on his violin, so I couldn't say for certain whether it was her prodigy or the piano itself he was jealous of. And Joanne was a prodigy. One of her teachers said it first, and although it was said with wonderment and pride, Joanne wore it like a burden, and I suppose it was a burden to study and play for so many years only and precisely because it would be wrong not to with such talent, because it would be a waste and something close to sin. I heard Joanne explain it to Melissa once, or try. In Joanne's version, prodigy was a diagnosis: a guarantee of burnout and decline, the accelerator you floor even though the brakes are shot and the bridge is out. She said it meant waking up one day as powerless to play as if you had never played at all, and Melissa took her literally. Worse, Joanne said she had known it was coming, that she'd been braced for it for years. And whether she was unwilling or exhausted or actually unable, she stopped playing except at Christmas and only then because I pressed her, and if she could have, she would have packed my piano away in the basement as deep among the boxes as Garfield had buried his violin.

It was all chosen for her, the piano and the organ, and all because Garfield had felt slighted with his violin and had nursed that hurt until he had a family of his own and could buy a piano and insist that his daughters both play it. He never understood that it was only his interminable vying with Helen that had landed him with that fiddle in the first place, that his sister Helen was older and was already playing the piano and Lillian realized she'd have one less argument to listen to each day if Garfield were set to playing something else. He even said it would be to

Lee's advantage to have Joanne to listen to, seven years older and seven years farther along. He never allowed as how that would intimidate a child who, like her mother, was not so much gifted as merely good. We could have afforded a second instrument for Lee, a flute or a cello. There was no need for economy. The punch line, of course, is that Lee is somehow the one who never stopped playing.

When she moved into a new house several years ago and wanted a better piano, I wrote a check for the one she'd picked out. I then sent a check in the same amount to Joanne with a note telling her I'd bought Lee a new piano, and Joanne wrote back saying she'd bought a set of prints with the money. It made no difference to me what she spent the money on, except that with Lee I had the pleasure of hearing her play on a good instrument, and with Joanne there was a lecture about the age and importance of the prints, their frames to admire, each caption to inspect, when all I wanted was to remind her they were no older than my own grandmother and couldn't I please sit down, even if it was on that modern horror she called a sofa.

Of course, Garfield could have taken up the piano at any time. I could likely have shamed him out of his chair if I'd gone in and offered to teach him myself. That would have been something, Garfield Maguire practicing scales. But he would only have said that that wasn't what he wanted at all, that he'd given up music entirely when he gave up the violin, and that everything had been spoiled and his only enjoyment now was in listening, when in actual fact taking up the piano would have deprived him of his defining grudge, and left him on view as an amateur, besides.

Garfield rode Joanne and rode her. If she was asked to play the organ at mass, he crowed about it to anyone who would listen, but then would turn and tell her not to worry, he'd arranged an extra lesson with her organ teacher so she wouldn't embarrass herself. Garfield left me alone when I sat down to the piano, but then he likely had such low expectations and such a low opinion of my playing that Joanne and I might have been playing different instruments altogether. Each hour Joanne spent playing at home passed like a punishment, and for what I never knew, although it was clear that Gar felt entitled, obligated even, to fashion Joanne into a version of himself he hadn't achieved the first time around. He was always on hand to tell her what to learn and how, and whether he had any expertise in the matter himself was none of her concern. He instructed her and he quizzed her, and couldn't do a thing as simple as look down at the Mississippi from atop a bluff without holding forth about glaciers and the Pleistocene and the black chernozem soil they had left around us.

There hasn't been another three-year-old in all of history who knew the word chernozem, I told him, but he took that as praise and looked out at the islands that rose out of the rushing water as if it had all been his idea somehow, as if he had been the one to let the glacier out of the gate. It's little wonder Joanne gave up the piano as soon as she decently could.

I suppose I could have gotten him to lighten up if I'd given in to temper, if I'd yelled and stomped right there in the living room, but I was too lady-like for that, too unwilling to lower myself with bad behavior, and Garfield knew it. He helped me to believe that he was quicker and smarter than I was, too, so there would have been no use in reasoning, either. He'd only have turned it on me and had me sputtering in seconds, defending myself and insisting that I believed in discipline as much as he did and the parent's duty to supervise. And it did no good to simply play the piano myself and be seen to enjoy it. He'd listen to my show tunes and thank me for my pleasant little concert and miss my point entirely each time. It did no good to coax Porter and Estelle into playing when they were visiting, either. And if we played together, and heaven help us if we sang, Garfield would smile and shake his head. We were too silly, too incorrigible. Look what he had to put up with. And our poor mother; clearly, we'd been at this for years. Garfield never knew that the sweet little song Porter played with a wink to me before he'd let someone else have a turn at the piano was my song, Maggie's Song, that he'd composed for me and told me was our secret, since he couldn't think of anything for Estelle.

I was Maggie, swinging my legs on the piano bench next to Porter, and then I was Margaret for years and years. I'm Margaret still, and I sit alone at my kitchen table in the evening with the paper and my coffee, and I have the radio going over there on the counter because I'm not reading the paper, I'm just turning pages. I can't read the news anymore, I need to have it told to me, because without the radio going I hear the piano still and Garfield's voice. I hear Joanne playing until he clears his throat or blows his nose or tells her to start over or play that last bit again. I can close my eyes or keep them open, I can listen or not to the radio. It makes no difference. And if I go into the living room and sit on the davenport, there's the piano to my left and the green chair and ottoman across from me, and I see Joanne and Garfield both, and Garfield isn't looking at her, his eyes aren't even open, and still he's telling her, It's always pained me that you have to wear glasses, Joanne, and such heavy ones. And Joanne stops her playing and lays her glasses on top of the piano, and when she continues it's from memory, because she can no longer see the notes, and he crosses his feet on the ottoman and tells her, Turn on the lamp, Joanne. You'll hurt your eyes.

·—25—·

here was always the fish to get through on Friday nights, the Catholic food we all ate regardless of which church each of us actually attended, and Lee to discipline throughout the meal for her pushing and poking at it, for the scornful curl of her lip. I filled the space around the fish with her favorites, with mashed potatoes and glazed carrots. I smiled and offered to race her and talked about dessert, but I couldn't remember a Friday when it hadn't ended badly. It always turned on a dime: dessert would switch from reward to punishment, a thing promised or revoked, depending on Lee's performance with the fish, and Garfield compounded it all by becoming more mercurial at dinner each year during Lent. Chin up! he'd tell Lee one night, Easter's coming, and then no more fish until next year! only to treat her to a lecture the next evening on duty and family, sin and redemption, and heaven and hell. Even Garfield seemed to know that we were walking a tightrope, though, and after a rigorous lecture when Lee had been required to sit alone at the kitchen table and keep her uneaten fish company for an hour, he'd sent her to bed early but then softened and played cards with her in her room until bedtime, leaving Lee thinking she'd won without understanding what it was she'd won exactly, or why.

We went to church, all of us together, twice each Easter Sunday. St. Paul's early, with a stop at a café downtown for breakfast before we went on to the ten o'clock service at Grace Church. Neither Lee nor I would eat any breakfast at home Easter morning, out of respect for Gar and Joanne, who were fasting, and if Lee didn't fuss about it, I would slip her a cookie or two when the others weren't looking. She finally asked why we had to go to both churches the year she was seven, the last Easter that Garfield was alive. She was standing on the coffee table in her socks while I pinned up the hem of her Easter dress. She said it to the room at large, not to either one of us in particular, but after Garfield met my eyes from across the room, he raised his newspaper again and snapped it a little to let me know he was excusing himself from the conversation. He was still listening, of course, and I imagined he'd dipped his chin so he could look over the tops of his reading glasses at a blurry page and listen that much better.

We started doing that even before we were married, I said. It's the only way we can be in church together at Easter.

I turned her a quarter turn on the table. Hold still, I told her, or it'll be all cattywampus.

Am I turning Catholic, Mom?

Garfield coughed at that one and snapped his paper hard, and if I'd had any pins in my mouth right then, I'd have spit them out for sure.

Forevermore! What put a notion like that into your head? Surely not the fish!

Joanne was still washing our dinner dishes and couldn't hear us, and her clattering and the noise from the running tap had emboldened Lee. I could feel her weighing it, though, hefting the repercussions before she finally said, No, not that. Saying the rosary at night with Joanne.

Garfield stayed behind his paper and I kept pinning. You wouldn't have known this was news to either one of us.

I said, You're still Presbyterian, the same as I am, and I waited.

I knew that Garfield was waiting, too, to see if the next thing out of Lee's mouth was a reminder that she'd been baptized in Latin at St. Paul's, just like her sister, just like her father. I couldn't remember for the life of me whether we'd ever told Joanne, and I decided, when Lee said nothing more, that we clearly had not. Joanne could never have resisted that one if she'd known, the chance to tell Lee that technically she was also Catholic, which would have left Garfield unable to leave off explaining that technically Lee was excommunicate and a heretic besides. I pinched a clump of pins between my lips and Garfield kept his ankles crossed on the ottoman and turned a page as if nothing of interest had happened at all.

I waited until the girls were in bed and then motioned to Garfield with my head. He followed me through the kitchen, but when I reached his office, I changed my mind and led him down to the basement, to put as much distance between our voices and the girls' ears as I could. I crossed my arms and raised both eyebrows and waited for him to speak.

I had nothing to do with this, Margaret, he said.

I didn't think that you did. I still want to know what you're going to do about it.

We'd been hurtling toward this moment since the day Gar told me to just go ahead and take Lee to church with me, and actually it had started long before that when the two of us had said, *Yes, of course,* to a priest or two when they laid out the conditions for our marriage, and we'd thought it would be smooth sailing after that. Agreeing to a thing and then carrying it out are disparate acts, and agreeing to a thing and then flouting it right under the eyes of the people you made your promise to is foolhardy. The priests at St. Paul's all knew that Garfield had two daughters—they'd poured their water over both of them— and they knew that only one of them was both present with him each week in church and enrolled in the church grade school next door. We'd gone unchallenged, and I suppose we both thought we'd gotten away with it, and here was Joanne trying to correct the situation from inside our own home.

It's only a set of prayers, he said.

You of all people should know that it's not. *We* don't say the Hail Mary, *we* don't have a cult of Mary.

Is this really something we need to argue about?

You make it sound like we're squabbling over the Easter ham.

I will speak to Joanne, he said.

And what will you say?

He had a hand on the bannister already and one foot on the bottom stair. He said, I have no idea. I'll let you know when I've said it.

I could have gone back upstairs with him, but I let him walk up alone. I watched him and saw for the first time the way he pulled himself up by the bannister as much as he lifted himself with each step. When had he become so earthbound, so slow? I shook my head. I wished I hadn't just seen what I'd seen or heard what he had said. He had divided us again, and the most I could hope for was to talk to Lee.

He told me later that he'd given Joanne permission to continue, reasoning that it was part of Lee's education. She might as well be conversant with the Rosary, he said, if half of her relatives were Catholic. He neglected to say, though, how long he thought this might take, and whether he thought he'd recognize the tipping point between acquaintanceship and adherence. It was clear to me that Garfield was adrift, although he would never have said so, and when I first went into the hallway in my stocking feet to listen outside their door, he didn't say a thing.

They never knew I was there, I'm sure of that. I made a point of turning right after the hall door so that it would look to them, if they saw me peripherally, if they were watching for me at all, like I had simply gone into Garfield's and my bedroom. I even pushed our door open a little more, just for the hiss of the door skimming the carpet, before I went back slowly and stood closer to their open door. I could picture them well enough without seeing them. The yellow lamplight falling sideways across their faces, the beads flashing, Lee's eyes open wide, and Joanne's head bowed with the gravity of it all.

In nomine Patris, et Filii, et Spiritus Sancti, Amen.

It was both of them together. Lee was a quick learner. I wondered if Joanne required her to cross herself, as well.

Credo in Deum Patrem omnipoténtem, Joanne said.

What does omnipotent mean?

I already told you. It means all-powerful.

Garfield came into the hall then with a finger to his lips. He walked past me and leaned into the girls' room to say, No more than one decade tonight, and then walked past me again into the living room as if I hadn't been standing there at all.

They kept at it all through Lent. Garfield told me to let them be on the nights he wanted to keep me from listening in the hall. He'd say that he'd told them to keep it short, but one night I finally had my fill and burst in on the girls. It would have been easier, I thought, to simply send both girls off with Garfield on Sundays and attend my own church alone. The loneliness and the looks of sympathy I'd have had to bear would have been easier than this. And I'd done it all while trusting Gar, never speaking to my own minister, never questioning my own heart, just stumbling forward with blind belief in my husband's opinions. But the night I stood in the hall and heard Lee ask, Why do I have to do this? and Joanne said it was because Lee was turning seven soon and that seven was the Age of Reason, the age when she'd know right from wrong, I wept at what Garfield's recklessness had brought us to.

That's not a reason, Lee said. I already know what's right and what's wrong.

And when Lee asked again, Why do I have to do this? and I heard Joanne's answer, I went in and snatched the rosaries out of their hands. I put Joanne's rosary in its box on the nightstand and Lillian's rosary in my pocket. No more, I said, and then I collected myself enough to say good night before I went and dropped Lillian's rosary on the table beside Garfield in his chair, wondering if he'd heard the last thing Joanne said before I rushed in to stop them, wondering if he'd heard her tell Lee, Because I don't want you to go to hell.

I woke earlier, when it was still dusk and the tips of the bare trees were red like the heads of matches aflame. I wake again and it's dark. My curtains are still open. There is light coming in at the bottom of my door. I hear Melissa's voice. She's on the phone in the hallway, trying to speak quietly. I wonder if it's Joanne or Lee on the other end. She puts the phone in the cradle and opens my door. The light falls in across my bed and she can see me well enough to see that I'm breathing. I suppose she doesn't see that I'm awake because she closes the door again, and then I hear her in the kitchen, opening the refrigerator, opening drawers. I don't know what time it is, and I don't care enough to roll over and look at my clock. It isn't that late if Melissa is still up. I'm happy listening to her move around the house and I just stare out my window.

I have all the time in the world these days. There isn't a thing I need to do anymore but it's been thought of already and done for me. I sleep, I wake, I accept meals. I give the tray a little push as it's being lifted away again. I say thank you. I still take myself to the toilet, and I wash what needs washing at the bathroom sink. Melissa gets my bottle of Jergens and does my legs and feet for me. She takes a little extra for her hands each time and tells me the scent makes her think of me. Life is bookended with this kind of repose. People doing for you. Seeing that you're toileted and fed, that you're content. They don't expect anything in return, only that you grow, or in my case finish growing old.

I believe it's all beginning to slip away. It would have left me crying before, but it isn't anything to cry about. It's something to prepare for, to wait for, and then when it's time to leave it isn't hard. It's simply time to leave. They say your loved ones come for you when you die, and if that's true there'll be a whole gang coming for me. Or maybe only one can come and the rest of them have to cool their heels, and I suppose then it should be Mother because I want to be the one to come for my girls when it's their time.

When Melissa was born, I wondered how much of her life I would even get to see. I felt a joy that was close to pain when I first saw her in Joanne's arms. My child holding her own child. I saw Joanne blindsided by love when she looked at her own daughter, before she could remember to be afraid. I'm not one of those who wants to live forever, but Melissa made me want as much as I could get, and now she's a woman herself, older than I was when I met Garfield, and she's caring for me.

I was still young and caring for Lillian when she died, and I remember thinking how disappointed she would have been to know that I had been the last one to speak to her in this world. I went in to her one morning to ask if she was up to coffee and found her dead by the time I went back with her cup. The sight of her stopped me cold before I even crossed the threshold. Her face was suddenly younger and she would have looked as if she were only sleeping except for the lack of a frown. I set her coffee cup on the bedside table and watched for her chest to rise or fall, waited for a pulse to throb among the cords of her neck. There wasn't a soul I could have said it to, but I was of two minds in that moment. She'd been a vexation to me for years. I hadn't once liked her, but there had been things about her I respected, like her intellect, and in that moment there was little I wouldn't have given to get her back again. Wife, mother, grandmother, teacher, child. No one would ever know all the things she'd had inside her.

I'd feel differently now, if I could stand by her deathbed again. I believe I'd feel glad for her, and I'd hope that it was her Ruth who would come to get her. Back then, of course, she only reminded me of my father's death and made me wonder whether my own mother wouldn't be far behind. That day, she left me feeling exactly as I did each spring when I watched the magnolia at the bottom of our yard and the way its petals, once they began to fall, fell faster than you could count them. Unlike the petals of other flowering trees, they fell before they faded, still turgid and cool, so that their lying on the ground became for me the most wretched loss of spring.

·—27—·

arfield died on a Sunday. A summer Sunday when I thought that all I had to worry about was sweat, whether I could get through church without damp patches showing on my dress, without soaking my hankie with dabbing at my neck.

The eggs for Lee's and my breakfast fluttered and spat in the pan, yolks humped up and the edges gone brown in the fat. Garfield went past me to the fridge to get the cold water jug. I saw the crease I had ironed into his shirtsleeve. I saw him hold his necktie against his belly with his other hand, to keep it from swinging out. I heard Joanne come in then, asking if she could stay home from church, and I turned towards her just because of the tone of her voice, before I even understood fully what she had said, laying the spatula down so I could feel her forehead.

She wasn't hot, she wasn't sick at all, but her eyes were pleading for me to be quick and help her.

Go on back to bed if you don't feel well, I said, but Garfield was there suddenly with his palm on her forehead, glowering and wanting to know if it was her stomach again, or a headache. Lee went past and he felt her head, too. Lee looked at me and I shook my head to tell her to be quiet and nodded toward her chair so she'd sit down. Joanne stayed standing, braced, back against the cabinets. I said that it was almost time for Garfield to leave if he didn't want to be late, but he wouldn't budge. He wanted to know precisely what was wrong with Joanne. Lee snorted but regretted it and began to swing her legs hard under the table, and Garfield had to know why.

She's not sick. She's sleepy, Lee said.

He sat down then with the glass of water he had poured for himself. Took a leisurely sip. There was no sound at all, no possibility of any of us speaking until Garfield had spoken first.

Who would like to tell me why Joanne is sleepy, he said.

She was reading again, Lee said. She had the light on all night.

I did not!

How long were you up last night, Joanne?

Lee scraped a fingernail on the raised pattern of leaves on her juice glass. I wanted to ask Gar how he could pretend to be surprised by Joanne's reading at night when we found him so many mornings asleep on the davenport with a volume of the *Britannica* open across his belly and all the lamps blazing.

Joanne! he barked, and I was sorry I hadn't spoken my mind.

Until three or so.

And you thought you could skip mass because you didn't get enough sleep.

I don't have to play or sing today.

Is music your sole responsibility at church? Have some water, and then get ready, he said. You and I are going to mass.

There was little point pretending there was more than one outcome to all of this, so when I said that they could go to 10:30 mass, I wasn't so much suggesting a nap for Joanne and a later service as I was trying to distract Garfield and make him holler at me, instead. But no, he and Joanne had responsibilities and obligations. Things you couldn't rearrange on a whim. Besides which, they'd have to wait longer to eat any breakfast.

I laid Lee's and my plates on the table. Both yolks had held. I should have burst one of them, I thought. I should have broken a yolk so I could play the martyr and take the ruined egg for myself and sulk and give Garfield the opportunity to show me, by example, how to behave reasonably.

Garfield glanced at my plate and looked back at Joanne. I'm not feeling any too well myself today, but I am going to mass, he said.

You said it was okay, Joanne nearly spat at Lee. You said the dark scared you.

Enough! Garfield yelled.

I looked at the coffee cup in my hands and listened to the chink of Lee's fork stabbing up a bit of bacon. Garfield was agitated. He straightened his back, then hunched forward, pulling sporadically at his necktie. Lee let a squeaky little fart and giggled into her orange juice. She looked sideways at me over her glass, knowing I would smile at her, and I did. I gave her a wink, but then caught Joanne, still standing over by the counter, looking back and forth, incensed, between Gar and me.

What, I said as flatly as I could to warn her that I knew what was coming, and that she should think two or three times and hold her tongue.

Isn't she going to excuse herself? Say excuse me!

Your father and I will discipline your sister, I said.

She can't just get away with that. She should be sent from the table.

I took hold of Lee's hand. I leaned forward to look as hard at Joanne as I could, to try to make her look away from Lee, and I said, Joanne, that horse is too high. Stop now, please, or you can leave the room.

She looked at me finally, just as wounded as I knew she would be, and before any sound could come out of her open mouth, Garfield slammed the table with his fist.

Enough! You heard your mother. That's all.

Lee had pulled all her hair forward, making a curtain she

could cry behind. I got up to take her from the room. Garfield yanked again at his necktie and rose from the table, pushing in his chair and then leaning on it like he was tired from running. He said, If we could get through just one morning in this house without bickering. He said it to himself, to the room, to the yellow smear I'd left on my plate. Get ready, Joanne. Right now.

Lee and I sat on the bed in the girls' room while we waited for them to go. I couldn't imagine what she was thinking and I knew she'd never tell me. She'd never get a complete sentence out past the choked crying that would start if she tried. I looked out the window when I heard the car on the gravel drive and, once they had turned onto Main, I took Lee out to finish her breakfast, but it had gone cold and I hardly blamed her when she didn't eat.

Go practice while I clean up, I told her. I smiled at her to let her know that practicing now would be the sneaky thing to do, that we'd get the better of Joanne and Gar if we could say she'd done her hour while they were at church. There would be no criticism, no eye-rolling when she hit the wrong keys. No one calling, Again! impatient for her to be more accomplished than she was. There would be time between Lee's Yankee Doodle and Joanne's Rachmaninoff.

Lee played and I cleaned, and when I was done I sat in the living room with my knitting until the screen door slammed again in the kitchen and Garfield was there, throwing his suit coat on a chair and twisting his head back and forth, pulling off his tie.

Call someone for a ride, would you, Margaret? he said.

It's perfectly clear to me, all these years later, how he looked standing there with his tie balled up in his fist, breathing hard and telling me the heat was too much for him. It's clear to me now that he was wincing because he was already in pain, even though I told myself then that he was just squinting because the sunlight outside had been so strong.

He said he'd be fine when I offered to stay home. He said he'd just sit and try to stay cool, so I went to call Mildred and catch her before she left the house. I asked Joanne to get Lee ready and then thought better of it and sent her to the kitchen to get Garfield some iced tea, instead. I could see the refrigerator door standing open from the hall where I stood with the telephone, and I knew Joanne was there on the other side of it, taking her time with the ice, getting as much cold air as she could before someone yelled at her to close the door.

I went into the coat closet for my hat and was still pinning it on as I went back through the living room. There Gar was in the green chair by the picture window with his eyes closed and his feet up on the ottoman, and there was Joanne with the iced tea in her hand, watching him and letting the glass slip lower and lower in her grasp. I let my hands fall from my hat with a slap against my dress so she'd stop with whatever nonsense she had thought up and just put the glass on the side table. I couldn't imagine why she'd want to startle and annoy him with a dropped glass and tea that needed soaking from the carpet, why she wouldn't rather just put the tea down and go to her room to read or sleep for an hour behind her closed door. I frowned at her, bewildered, and she put the glass down and left the room. I told Gar I'd make lunch when we got back from church, and he nodded without ever opening his eyes.

Mildred swayed Lee and me down the long drive to the street in her huge sedan, tires popping and crunching the gravel. I looked out the rear window to see if Joanne was waving, but she'd pulled her bedroom curtains.

The rest is imagination.

·—28—·

We were ready long before Porter and Frances arrived. Joanne and Lee sat on the davenport, and I sat in one of the wing chairs by the fireplace. Lee mimicked Joanne's posture: knees and ankles together, hands clasped atop her knees, but Lee's back was so hunched that her elbows rested in her lap. I exhaled and looked away before they could see my expression. A week ago, I would have told Joanne to relax and Lee to sit up straight. I would have told them it was exhausting, waiting for them to hear what I always seemed to be repeating, but all I wanted now was to lie down, for someone to tell me that the day was over and that, even if I couldn't remember it, that we had all been to the church and to the cemetery and that everyone else had gone home.

I pulled again at the wrists of my gloves and patted my brooch. The mantle clock's ticking was so loud I spun around to look at it, to see if it could possibly be the same clock we'd always had there or if someone had switched it. When I looked back at the girls they were watching me, each of them wary in her own way.

I told Lee, Remember to watch Joanne when we're in the church. Just do as she does and you'll be fine. I smiled feebly at them and then we heard Porter's car in the drive.

Why didn't he go all the way back to the garage? Lee wanted to know.

I asked him not to, that's why, I said. You don't leave for a funeral through the back door.

Porter came in with his hat in his hand and said, Estelle came with us. Frances says she'll drive your car if you'd rather not sit six in ours.

But before I could tell him that was fine, Estelle was there pushing past him, rustling in her black polished cotton, looking for all the world as if she'd only misplaced her martini. That wasn't fair and I knew it. She was distressed, and wearing too many rings and too much lipstick was simply her way of distracting herself. She cupped the girls' chins in her hands and ran her fingers over their hair. Joanne, I knew this dress would hang on you, she said. Can't we tighten up this belt?

It looks worse if it's tighter.

Never mind then. It's fine. And, Sappo! I should have known you wouldn't have a veil. Here, switch with me.

She started to unpin her hat with its netting and straw flowers, but I stopped her.

I don't need any veil, Estelle. Keep your hat.

But what if you cry?

Well, then I'll wipe my eyes, I suppose. Now let's go.

The street was already lined with parked cars when we got to St. Paul's, and there were people on the sidewalk and on the steps of the church. Joanne craned to look while Porter parked the car. Frances patted her knee and said, They're all here for your father, honey, and I saw the thought forming in Joanne's eyes when she looked past me, bewildered, out the window, and even though the same thought was forming in my head, I couldn't stop her in time, or didn't stop her, and she said, But there are so many.

The funeral mass passed in pieces for me. I had come to St. Paul's occasionally with Lee, but only to hear Joanne play or sing, and she had always been in the choir loft then, never beside me in the pew. I made Lee cry when I stopped her from kneeling with her sister.

But you said to watch Joanne, she whispered.

Not that. When she kneels, we sit.

I put my hand on Lee's back and pushed gently until she leaned forward. We all had to lean forward, all of us except Joanne, because of the people in the pew behind us who were kneeling with their hands folded on the back of our pew. Five Presbyterians and a Catholic in a pew. Garfield would have howled at the profanity of it. I realized Joanne was crying, too, that her neck had gone red, and I thought that I never could have guessed it would be humiliation that made both of them cry in the church instead of sorrow.

Joanne couldn't yet realize what a mess her father had landed her in. I had only just begun to understand, myself. She'd be the only Catholic in our family now, bereft of both her father and someone to sit with during Sunday mass. There was no more possibility of her attending Grace Church with Lee and me from now on than there was of our switching to St. Paul's. Even suggesting such a thing, merely as a practical measure, would be seen by either church as repudiation. We'd made our pew, you could hear them say, and now we could pray in it.

Frances was quiet down at her end of our pew, folding and refolding her handkerchief. Estelle was sniffing behind her veil, and Porter had cleared his throat too many times, but it was Lee who shocked me, the way she cried soundlessly, never gasping or shuddering when she drew in breath, but still crying hard enough that her face and neck were wet. That she knew how to do that, that she had taught herself to cry like that, probably at night in the bed with Joanne, amazed me so that I forgot myself and gasped aloud when the priest sprinkled holy water at the casket and it hit me on the face.

When the mass was over, Estelle and Frances each held one of the girls by the shoulders where we stood at the back of the church with the priest. I was aware that someone was holding me too and that it had to be Porter. I knew that he was literally holding me up and that Estelle and Frances were doing the same for the girls when a tall, thin woman came up to me and said, Hello, Margaret.

I should have remembered that Helen was coming, I had asked Estelle to telephone her with the news myself, but once the slip of paper with Helen's phone number was in Estelle's pocketbook, I stopped thinking about it. I was used to not thinking about Helen. In the years since Lillian had died and she and Gar had argued, we had behaved as if Garfield had no living relations other than us. It had been ten years since I'd seen her last, and she had aged more than that. Her mouth was trembling, and her eyes were red and damp. She had come all the way from Ft. Lauderdale to stand in front of me at a funeral and say hello.

Good Lord, Helen, I said, and she smiled and said, Yes, good Lord.

When she looked at the girls, I felt Porter squeeze my shoulders. Everything had slowed for me and I couldn't think past what was happening right in front of me, but he remembered Helen and he saw Jamie standing behind her and saw what would happen when Helen spoke.

She touched Joanne's cheek and looked down at Lee and said, I'm your Auntie Helen, and this is your cousin Jamie.

Joanne blanched. You look like Gran, was all she managed to get out, although she might well have also said that Jamie looked just like Gar. We were looking at ghosts, every one of us, because Helen stopped smiling and told Joanne, You look like Ruth.

Helen hadn't turned precisely into Lillian, but her hair had gone white and her eyes had the intensity of Lillian's gaze. I could hardly stand to look at Jamie, who was right about the age that Garfield had been when I met him. He had Gar's black hair, combed straight back off his forehead, Gar's mouth, and those same flashing eyes. I heard Porter ask if they had a car and was shocked out of my staring by Jamie's voice, which was mercifully nothing like Gar's, saying that they did, and that they'd see us at the cemetery. But then I stared at Helen again and realized that Joanne, Lee, and I were the only ones still named Maguire, and that Helen and I were both widows, each of us carrying a dead man's name. I felt as if I would collapse right there where I stood, and I must have wobbled because Porter pressed my shoulders hard and turned me toward the door.

I had no recollection of what the priest said at the gravesite or even how I got there. I could only see the grave open in front of me and wonder how they dug it so absolutely straight and who had decided that plumb lines and right angles were most appropriate to death. Why couldn't it be ragged? Why shouldn't it look raw as a wound, as if, barehanded, someone had torn the earth apart?

The priest was shaking my hand; it was time to go. I thanked him. Garfield's coffin waited next to the grave. I wondered whether that was the patch of ground that was set aside for me. Joanne was beside me, staring at the coffin with a look I had never seen before. I took hold of her arm and said, Time to go, but she said, Not yet.

I handed Lee to Estelle and said in a low voice, It's time now. Everyone is waiting for us.

No, Joanne said. She yanked her arm away from my hand, but I took it back harder by the wrist so that when she struggled again she couldn't get loose. She began to shout, No! Please, no! and I held onto her and tried to hold her still so it wouldn't look as if we were fighting.

They have to lower the casket, I said. I felt panicked, holding on to her like that, and I half wondered if I was trying to get her to come with me or to prevent her from jumping into the grave.

I want to stay and watch them do it.

That's not done, Joanne. Please come with me now. That's simply not done.

She was panting and her voice was too loud. She said, I want to see for myself. I don't want to go until they've put him in the ground.

I said, No! You're making a scene. There are people waiting for us. We have to go.

Joanne dug in her heels and leaned away from me so that I was all that was holding her up, but Porter was there behind us suddenly and he took hold of her. It looked as if he were only comforting her, but he had hold of her firmly and pulled her back up on her own feet again.

Let go, he told me. I've got her. Come, Joanne.

He never let go, and he steered her between the trees and the older graves, back to the lane and the line of parked cars. People had stopped to watch, and I heard him tell Joanne to keep her head up and just look ahead at the cars. I looked at the back of Porter's head and nothing else and realized that Frances had me by the hand. I couldn't see where Estelle or Lee were, and I just had to keep walking.

Poor child, someone muttered as I passed. She can't bear to leave him.

·—29—·

 he woman, Mrs. Witherell I suppose I should say, wanted badly to march past me and into the house, as if she had a right as a member of St. Paul's to the residue of Gar's life, the small matter of his widow and daughters notwithstanding. Her eyes flicked over and past me into the living room. I wondered what she'd say if I told her, take it, just take it all. We heathens don't need much, not coffee tables or floor lamps, and heaven knows we don't need china or silver because we eat with our hands. I couldn't account for those greedy eyes, as if I'd read the will wrong and hadn't realized that Gar had left everything to his church. She'd come to the front door, too: the imposter's mistake. Any friend of Gar's or mine would have known our front door was a family joke. We came and went at the back.

She put a foot up on the step, hoping manners would prevail and I'd let her pass, but I kept hold of the open door with one hand and took hold of the frame with the other. Her eyes snapped past me once more and I guessed that Joanne or Lee or both had come into the room behind me.

I wanted to see how you all were, she said. A smile rolled briefly over her face, then she went back to looking past me. She was short and, standing on the porch, she could look directly under my outstretched arm.

That's very kind, I said. We're all doing as well as can be expected.

Are you getting hot meals? I'm sure you've had an avalanche of casseroles. Why, when my sister passed, her husband wouldn't have seen hot food again if it hadn't been for the neighbors. But I suppose it's different when the man passes, isn't it.

We're eating just fine. People have already come by from St. Paul's and from our church. I leaned a little on the word *our* to let her know she wasn't wanted, that she was late to the party.

She said, I saw Joanne down at the Beauty Academy today.

I waited; it wasn't a question. That unnerved her, and when she spoke again, she sputtered.

Why, I can't imagine that's very interesting for a girl of her intelligence. Is it your intention that she continue?

Yes, it is, I said. She's begun and she's going to finish.

But Garfield always said she was going to college! He said she was going to study dentistry—

He wanted her to study both. He wanted her to have a second profession to fall back on.

Well! She was all feigned admiration then and even clapped her hands together for emphasis. Doesn't that sound just like him, she said. Always an idea, always a plan.

I could have let her in then and sat her down in the kitchen where it was cooler. I could have taken her hat and poured iced tea and let the glasses sweat on the oilcloth while I told her I had also been aghast at the idea of Joanne's giving permanent waves and manicures, and that everyone could be sure Joanne was aghast as well. I could have given that woman a bona fide earful to take back with her to St. Paul's. I was incandescent with rage at Gar for dying and I would happily have scorched the ears clean off her head with a whisper of Gar's appetites and petty cruelties.

She stared at me bluntly as if she knew I was about to give in;

her eyes contracted and the corners of her mouth lifted the tiniest bit with pleasure.

Isn't it hot today? she said. I swear my dress collapsed the moment I put it on.

I remembered that the girls were watching all of this behind me, and gave her an unconvincing smile. My patience was petering out and she was beginning to look agitated, so I took a step closer to the doorframe and pulled the door against me to block her view.

I imagine you'll need help with things, she said.

I raised my eyebrows tolerantly. She was going to spell it out with no help from me.

Garfield's clothes and things, she said. His equipment. I thought I should offer, since I belong to St. Paul's.

That's kind, I said again. But I've had offers of help from my own church and someone has already asked to buy his equipment.

I stepped back and started to close the door, done, and happy to be done, with being polite. I'd given her a tale of rudeness to take with her instead. She could report that I'd cracked the door shut in her face and gone back to the pressing business of indoctrinating Joanne into Protestantism, but she stopped the door with her hand and said, I wondered about that correction.

I faltered then, as she must have known I would. I drew myself up and gave her a shaming look to let her see that I had believed people would be too embarrassed to ask, too averse to hearing anything as grubby as personal business firsthand and would wait instead for it to pass through other people's hands and pick up a gossip's sheen.

What a strange thing to get wrong, she said, and a smug smile, a grim little thing, twisted itself onto her face. She folded her hands and we both knew I couldn't possibly close the door now.

I smelled it, too, the thing she was poking at, and I was shamming when I said, My brother made a mistake. He misunderstood Joanne. It was all very confusing at the time.

Well, I'm beginning to think I should write my own obituary in advance, so it doesn't happen to me. Although you can't know a thing like that in advance, can you. Imagine, her getting something like that wrong, not knowing if she was with him or not when he died!

You spoke to Joanne? I said it sharply, loud enough that I heard my voice carry even as I shut the door in her face. There it was. It wasn't my china she was after, it was a look at our laundry she'd wanted, a jab with a long stick at all our dirty drawers. I knew when I slammed the door that I'd only confirm that we were hiding something, but I couldn't stand her smirking at me, knowing my face was guilty and confused, and I couldn't let her see that and wonder why it was both.

When I turned around, Lee was this side of blubbering, and Joanne looked as stricken as if I'd caught her with a bag of money and a smoking gun.

Did she ask you questions today? I said. I was still angry when I said it and Joanne couldn't do any more than stare at me, her face going red and her eyes filling up. She couldn't even manage to nod or shake her head no. She'd already decided it was somehow her fault that Mrs. Witherell had interrogated her, and I'd gone and confirmed it by turning in anger without stopping to explain who it was I was angry at, or why.

I breathed out and dropped my hands from my hips and told them both to go and splash cold water on their faces. When they turned together toward the bathroom in the hall, I pictured the fracas they'd have, each trying to take command of the sink and told Lee to go use the sink in the office, but she gave me a pleading sort of look I hadn't seen before and I relented, telling her to let Joanne have a turn first.

I was adrift, I realized, fully and irretrievably adult now, and all because of the word *widow*. Many times I'd felt a fraud, marveling that people found it reasonable that Maggie Doud was someone's wife and someone else's mother. But this was different; this all felt as if Garfield had whipped the horse and dropped the reins just to see how I would manage. The only thing I could think to do was to keep the girls fed and calm and hope we'd keep our wits until I knew how I'd proceed without him.

I found I could not do the simplest things without becoming enraged. If I opened the refrigerator, I saw the two hard-boiled eggs I'd made for him that he'd never gotten around to eating and that I still hadn't managed to throw out. In our closet, his suits and shirts still hung to the right of my things, which only reminded me that his laundry still lay bunched in its own basket in the basement because I had decided that would be less wretched somehow than mixing his things one last time in a wash with ours. I'd taken to sitting in one or the other of the wing chairs in front of the fireplace rather than sitting alone on the davenport, but even then I could never manage to look out the window or even at the piano and, when I looked at the davenport with its Garfield-shaped depression, all I could see was him stretched out along it, groggy with jug wine.

It was astonishing, the number of mundane objects he had owned, and more astonishing to see how quickly a toothbrush became a relic in need of a glass case. I could keep it all, I knew, keep it dusted and adopt an indifferent smile when people inevitably began to think me odd. Or I could give it all away, rush ahead without forethought, without recourse, and force a new situation. If there was a middle ground, I hadn't thought of it, but the visit from the Witherell woman convinced me I'd be gaped at with something more than pity from now on, no matter what I did.

It was still hot, so I laid a cold supper, just put everything on the table so each could take what she wanted. Butter and bread, ham slices and lettuce, cottage cheese, and celery and carrot sticks splayed like flower stalks in a glass of water. I started to get out the hard-boiled eggs, thinking I'd put them out halved and salted, but then realized none of us would eat them, knowing they'd been cooked for Gar, and I put the one back so hard in its bowl I flattened the side of its shell.

I realized, too, as I set things out, that the image of Joanne cornered by Mrs. Witherell was the first thought through my head that had been robust enough to displace the image of Garfield, dead on the waiting room floor. I could only imagine what they made of Joanne down there at the beauty school now, still by far the best student when it came to knowledge and tests and blindly following instructions, but now she came equipped with fingernails she'd chewed to ribbons and hair she'd stopped doing anything more with than putting a bobby pin on the one side to keep it out of her eyes.

I watched Joanne laying ham on her bread and felt as if I'd never seen her before. Not as if I were seeing her afresh or seeing something new, but as if I'd never known her at all. It had been alarming and a wonder when she started turning into a woman. Nearly as tall as I was suddenly, hips and breasts erupting overnight. I had thought it was all right, that this was more or less how she would look for the rest of my life, and that there would be time to get used to it, even to become inattentive to it and then marvel that old photos proved she had been small once and unfinished. But now her face had regressed and the child's hurt it wore did not match the length of her arms or the circumference of her head. This would become part of the whole. A layer she attached as she built outward from her core. It was the reverse of what I felt was happening to me: as if grief were peeling at my skin, not painfully, but like an onion, diminishing irreparably as its petals of flesh were pulled away.

What are you doing? I said. She was rocking in her chair.

My blouse is sticking. Can't you hear it?

Please stop, I thought, and looked at Lee who was sitting straight and still, who would normally, at seven, have been the one to be distracted by the varnish on her chair back catching at her sweaty blouse. I shook my head in answer and she stopped. I held my iced tea glass against one wrist, and then the other.

You don't have any vegetables, either one of you. Go on, I said. They're not going to eat themselves.

I imagined it would be Lee who would forget first, one day, that we were grieving and that grieving people don't chatter at meal times. She would tell me something funny she'd seen at school, and we'd be stopped cold that first time, having let something normal and pleasant happen.

Joanne scraped the last of her cottage cheese back and forth across her plate. She breathed in suddenly and sat straight, then frowned and slumped back in her chair.

Land sake! I said. Can't you sit still? I'm wrung out just watching you.

Do I need to keep going to beauty school?

Need to keep going? Why on earth not?

I'll have to go two more summers after this one to be certified, and we'd have to keep paying the tuition.

We have the money, Joanne, and your father wanted you to do this. Isn't that enough?

I stacked our dishes in the sink, but when I turned on the faucet the stream hit a fork lying on the top plate and spattered my hand and arm with hot water. The shock of it made me hiss, and as I shook my hand over the sink I heard Joanne saying that she didn't want to be a beautician.

You don't ever have to be a beautician, I told her, drying my arm with the dishtowel. You and Lee are both going to college. But this way, if anything should happen to me, you'll at least be able to take care of yourself.

Don't say that, please.

It's the truth. I'm sorry it's hard, but it is the truth.

The truth of it, though, was that I was afraid. I couldn't let Joanne quit the school because it was one of the few things left to pull us forward. It was Garfield's plan, and even if it was patently absurd and even insulting to Joanne, it was something we could carry out and and say that she had finished. I looked at Lee, staring at the place her plate had been, and wondered if we were doing anything at all that had been my idea. Certainly not the business of going to different churches, not even the girls' piano lessons, which I had opposed, at least in Lee's case. It was unfair that I would have to continue to drive us to two services every Sunday, and it was unfair that Joanne was going to waste time learning to give permanent waves.

Is this because of Mrs. Witherell? I asked her, and although she shook her head, I didn't believe her. I wish I could go there for you. I do, I told her. I wish I could go in your place until this all dies down, because it will die down. I promise you that.

Joanne's face was wretched; she couldn't meet my eyes. If she had, it would have been impossible for me to continue to pretend that I didn't know what was wrong. That I didn't know, truly, deeply, what it was she couldn't say, because she had said it once and I had pretended that I hadn't understood. So I looked away from her then, so she wouldn't see my eyes, so she wouldn't see that I had decided to continue to pretend.

If people wonder about the obituary, I told her, and if they're ill-mannered enough to ask you, you just say it was a mistake. Uncle Porter made a mistake. He thought you said that your father was alone when he died, so he wrote it that way, and then I corrected it.

But people think there's something wrong with that, Joanne said. They think that if there was a correction it means that we're hiding something.

There isn't anything to hide, I said. It's all there in the correction. He couldn't have been alone because you two had come home from church together. Lee and I were the ones who were gone.

I can't say that. I can't say that. She said, and sat hugging herself and rocking again in her chair.

I slapped the dishtowel into the sink, right into the dishwater, and I didn't care that it splashed me. She would not let it be, she would not let it be, and I wanted to snatch the plates out of the water and smash them one by one.

I got the bucket from the pantry instead, and set it on top of the dirty dishes to fill. I dumped in ammonia and a sponge and went through the kitchen door, through the back entrance way, and opened the door to the examination room.

What are you doing? Joanne yelled from the kitchen. Her voice was as panicked as if I was about to stick a broom handle in a hornet's nest.

I put the bucket down and went back into the kitchen. I'm going to clean the office, I said, and I took the broom and the string mop off their hooks on the pantry wall. It hasn't been cleaned yet, and you can help me.

Please don't make me.

There's a dentist downtown who wants to buy your father's equipment and I can't let him have it dirty. You can clean the waiting room.

I can't go in there.

Yes, you can.

She was defying me, or trying to. I didn't know whether to

scream or cheer. She would never have attempted it with Gar-field, but there she was, wild-eyed with terror and staring me down. I felt as if I'd stuck my finger in a light socket, certain that my hair was on end and that sparks would shoot from my fingers if I unballed my fists. I realized then that neither Joanne nor Lee had ever truly listened to me, and that anytime they'd quibbled over a request that I had made, their father had been there to end it and make certain they obeyed, and I'd just proved it by telling Joanne she was going to finish beauty school precisely because her father had wanted her to.

We're going to clean these rooms, I said. There's nothing in there to scare you. You've cleaned in there countless times, and it needs it again.

I went through to the examination room and waited. Neither of them followed me, and when I went back again, yelling, Joanne, get in here! only Lee was still in the kitchen.

She ran away, Lee said, and I screamed Joanne's name. Lee followed me into the living room, where I turned in a circle as if I couldn't see everything in there all at once, as if it were possible somehow for Joanne to hide. Lee held onto the front of my dress and beat her thigh with a fist. I pulled my dress free from her hand and went into the bathroom, and after I had yanked the shower curtain back and Joanne wasn't there, I went into their bedroom, and then back into the hall. Lee followed me, but I pushed her away each time I turned so she couldn't catch hold of my dress again, so she couldn't trip me. She stopped chasing me when I turned toward the door of Gar's and my bedroom. There was no other place in the house Joanne could be.

Would she have believed me if I had said that, when I opened the closet door and saw her there beneath the dresses and the suits, her knees drawn up and her face in her hands, I saw myself?

That when I took hold of her by the front of her blouse and by her arm, it was me I pulled out of the closet and threw onto the floor?

My head cleared when I saw Joanne at my feet, curled in a ball with her arms around her head. I cried out and I sobbed and I pulled at my hair as if I truly would tear it out. I knew that Lee was in the doorway, crying open-mouthed, but I couldn't look at her. I sank to the floor with my legs splayed out and my back against the bed. I covered my mouth with both hands and screamed into them, and when I was able to drop them I said in a voice so calm it scared me, You weren't with him. I know you weren't with him at all.

Lee ran to me then and lay with her face in my lap, and I put one hand on her head and the other on Joanne's wrist, and I cried because neither of them pulled away. Neither of them flinched when they should have, because I was the monster and they were left with me.

I was the one who had chosen their father. I had married a man who deserved to die alone.

I thought of telling Joanne that it wasn't her house when she said she'd asked Evelyn Ehlers to come over here for a visit. I'm sure she saw the thought flash behind my eyes, then saw me blink and dismiss it, because she was right. Evelyn should come by. She's our neighbor, we all need to thank her, and if I am piqued, it has less to do with not being consulted first than with my now having to change out of my housecoat and into real clothes, when all I really want is to just slop around the house and be comfortable. So I let Joanne make the coffee and I watch her fan the cookies out in a ring on their plate, and when I allow myself a little laugh, she surprises me. She knows exactly why I'm laughing, and she's telling Melissa that I played cards every day at lunch with a fellow we called Brownie, and when it became common knowledge around the electric company that I was also beating him daily at Gin, that he was already fifty theoretical dollars in hock to me, he put an end to the ribbing he was getting by letting it circulate that I'd worked as a croupier in Vegas after the war. I never corrected the misapprehension, and it became a family joke. Anyone who'd considered the math would have realized that I was home with small children during and after the war, but if they wanted to imagine a different life for me, well, that was their business.

I raise an eyebrow at Melissa, at the way she's looking at me, and she grins. It's a plausible story, she's letting me know, and suddenly I wish Estelle were here. We could have gone to Vegas together, I'd tell her. Skipped the husbands and been a sister act at the tables, or better still, Estelle could have been the croupier, all charm and fresh lipstick, and I could have been a player. We might have made a tidy pile. And now I'm laughing again. I can see us telling Porter as clear as if it actually had happened, his looking at the two of us, suitcases in hand and headed for the depot. He'd have been all amazement. He'd have forgotten to hold the door or even to tell us to drop him a line. He'd never have made it up from the table, and been stuck muttering *Don't those two beat all?*

I'll have to do my daydreaming later. Evelyn's calling hello outside the kitchen door, and we're all on our feet. We've never hugged Evelyn before, but we're hugging her now and none of us has a hankie and Evelyn couldn't use one if she did because of the poinsettia and the tin of cookies she's holding. We're less effusive, back in the bright light of the kitchen, than we were in the hall, but Evelyn squeezes Joanne and Melissa's hands and says, I bet you're both glad to see Margaret looking so well. They are, they are, Joanne assures her, and it's all because Evelyn called the paramedics, but Evelyn doesn't see it that way.

Your mom called me first, she says, and she was having a heart attack when she did it!

We couldn't laugh about this with anybody else.

The coffee gets itself poured, and Evelyn takes a cookie to be polite, to give herself something to do while she's listening to Joanne tell all about the hospital and every doctor or nurse who touched me between that night and this day. It's too much, but Evelyn takes it all in, shakes her head and lets her eyes go wide at all the right moments. I suspect she knows that this is why she was invited: not so much so we could thank her, though that was certainly heartfelt, but because Joanne needed a new audience. She needed to tell it one more time. And whether because she's curious or because she knows how rare it is to find Joanne in a confessional mood, Evelyn starts asking questions.

How old were Joanne and Lee when Evelyn and her husband bought the property back of ours? How many years had our kitchen windows looked out at each other? What year was it again that Melissa was born? None of it's intrusive, but I wonder if Evelyn can have any idea how she's helping me. Joanne would say just about anything right now. Evelyn is not a relative, not quite a family friend, but her life and her property line have abutted mine for over thirty years, and that makes her our witness. She hardly knew Garfield, either, but that doesn't matter because she was the one who was there across the yard while we worked through the wobble in our legs those first months without him.

Melissa and I could turn to mist right now. I doubt Joanne would notice a thing. She's holding forth, completely in her element, and so far it's just facts. But now they're back to Garfield, and Evelyn asks how old Lee was when he died, and when Joanne says, Seven, and Evelyn says, That's too young to lose your father, we all of us shake our heads at the pitiful waste.

And then Joanne says it. She says, Lee was with him when he died, you know, and Evelyn is aghast.

No, she says, and she frowns because it's painful to hear, because suddenly it feels as if it happened just the other day. Evelyn doesn't look to me for confirmation—it must be true, Joanne has said it. And now Joanne is looking at the plate of cookies with her eyebrow in an eloquent arch, her face a genteel and sorrowful mask, and this is when I catch Melissa's eye and shake my head minutely before I look away again. This is the truth now. Joanne has said it aloud enough times, to Melissa, probably Bill, and now to a neighbor, that it seems she has come to believe it herself and can say it right here in my kitchen.

There's nothing to do then but ask after Evelyn's children and grandchildren. To thank her again for the poinsettia and the tin of cookies, to call Happy New Year! and wave her back across the snowy yard to her own back door. Evelyn's visit would have been different, easier even, if Lee had been here, but now at least I'm sure Melissa sees that Joanne constructed this version of the truth, and if she sees that much, she might also understand that it is an edifice designed to protect, if not absolve, Joanne from the weight of her own memory.

I have never told Joanne that there was nothing she could have done. I have never made her look at me and hear the words *He would have died, no matter what.* If she had run down the middle of our street screaming for help, if she had telephoned for an ambulance, her father would still have been dead before help arrived. I always told myself that this was beyond doubt, so obvious that it didn't need saying. But the truth of it is that saying that much would then have begged the question *Why didn't you go to him?* Why didn't you do the one thing you could have done, even though you were only fifteen and he was beyond help? I know now that I never said anything because she could have asked the same of me, should have asked, should have turned that question on its head and demanded my answer. *Tell me, Mom. Why didn't I go to him?*

I had thought all these years that saying nothing was the same as saying that I understood. That if she had denied him succor at the end, it was not done out of fear, but because it was what he had earned. But hadn't I only been absolving myself? Hadn't I been blaming only Garfield, who'd made Joanne worship and hate him, and not myself? I had chosen him, after all, so you could say that the fault all lay with me. It wouldn't have mattered a jot that Garfield Maguire was a bully if I had married another man.

We're left now with the rest of the day, with the time it will take for the words *Lee was with him* to stop pinging off the walls like some nightmare ball in an arcade game. I wonder which of us will be the first to speak again, now that it's just us. We might make it all the way to lunch. It will be something mundane but essential that breaks the silence, like what to have for dinner, or whether there are more paper towels in the basement, because the roll in the pantry is out.

I'm tired. I want not to be awake, not to think about this anymore. I want not to know that I have absolved myself in every possible way, not to wonder whether I was fooled by him, or if I only fooled myself. I want not to be in this tower in my fairy-tale forest, calling Joanne to come to the window of her own tower, telling her that she can chip away at the bricks like I'm doing and throw them to the ground. Telling her that Melissa is there to pick them up, although where she will take them and what she will build, I have no idea.

·—*31*—·

I take the roof off the house and look down inside. Joanne is in her room. She's stepped out of her dress and is lying on top of the covers in her slip. Garfield heaves up in the living room, and the armchair complains. He's not in control, it's clear. His feet are too heavy on the floor, and when he pushes open the door of his examination room, it swings too fast and bangs against the wall. Joanne's eyes open. Staring straight up, she hasn't moved, but every bit of her is alert to the wrongness of these sounds. When he upsets the tray of instruments and it crashes to the floor, her breathing goes shallow. She'd stop breathing entirely if she could, remove herself from whatever it is that's coming.

Garfield leans on his dental chair. He feels himself sinking, he's certain he should keep moving. He calls Joanne's name but hears nothing in return because she's still frozen on her bed, so he calls out again, Joanne, I need you. Croaking, sobbing, and nothing happens.

I have to decide when it is, precisely, that they both understand what is happening, and it seems clear that it is now: the moment when Garfield calls and she doesn't come. They've both guessed that he is dying and now Garfield also knows that Joanne will not come to him. That he cannot compel her, not for help or comfort. He doesn't bother to wonder if she didn't hear him because the house isn't that big, it isn't big at all, and only one door is closed between them. She'll never come to him, and there is nothing for either of them to do but wait.

Garfield has fallen now on the waiting room floor. It's the last thing he will do. He's on his side, looking at his hand in front of him on the linoleum. He doesn't know that Joanne has gotten out of bed and is looking at herself in the mirror above her dresser. He doesn't know that she has left her glasses on her nightstand so she won't be able to see herself clearly. She's shaking her head, she's gone white at the thought of what she is doing. She understands fully that it cannot be undone.

Joanne backs away from the mirror and then backs away some more, hoping that what she sees will become so blurred that it's no longer Joanne; neither Joanne's brown hair nor Joanne's ivory slip, but only shapes and colors, devoid of meaning or intent.

Garfield's eyes close and he's amazed that it's ending like this. It would surprise him, that this last cruelty was hers, except that he understands now what he is and what he has taught her to become.

I never could manage to erase this once I had seen it. Even though I know I only imagined it, it has always seemed true. I know this means that it is also the only truth I ever wanted, or the only truth that I could stand, but it has never altered, not in thirty-five years, and I am the only one who could have imagined it because I saw Joanne's face when we walked in through the kitchen door that day, when she knew her father was dead and I still did not.

·—32—·

*P*eople think that I'm visiting Gar when I go to Oak Grove, but I'm not. Not really. How much fascination could he hold, a name and two dates on a modest stone, and a miniature flag on Veterans Day? It's my own grave that draws me, the extra plots I bought in my widow's panic when he died. Which side of Gar will I be on? I've never known, never asked. I'll have my own little stone near his, that much I know, like Porter and Frances with their separate beds.

When Porter bought their family plot in Ft. Madison, it was decades early, and he only did it then because he had to, because Barbara Jean had died. He bought a large stone on which you could read Doud all the way from the curving drive. It wasn't ostentatious, but the sight of it surprised you until you realized he'd likely wanted something grander for the baby than he would have for himself. Barbara Jean would lie there alone for nearly forty years before Frances died and could be laid beside her. Porter could have had no way of knowing which of them would join her first or how soon, so he'd wanted something there to say that he and Frances were coming. Something more than just one pitiful little stone that told that Barbara Jean Doud had done her living and her dying in the space of six months.

I had bought no such family stone to say Maguire. It wasn't my name and it never occurred to me to do so, even though I had Porter's example before me. I planned to have a simple stone like Gar's, and I realized only later that, without a family stone as a beacon, our graves might one day look like the strangest of coincidences. By comparison to Porter and Frances, I had not broadcast that we were a family, but just two people, surname of Maguire, who happened to be buried in adjacent plots. And in the first days after Gar's death, in my worst distress and confusion, I had signed a contract for the deed to four plots. I had bought plots for the girls, as well, and what I was thinking there, I have no idea. That this was ridiculous hit me first in St. Paul's, the day Joanne and Stephen were married. Lee would be married too one day, there was no reason to doubt that, and there I was, staring wide-eyed past the priest and all the proceedings, wondering how I was meant to plant six people in a patch of ground marked out for four, never mind all of my unborn grandchildren.

You could say that when I go to Oak Grove I'm practicing, and in a way of course, I am. If I'm going to lie there for all eternity, I want to know the place. Looking up, I want to know how the trees, those particular trees, sound when the wind moves through them, how their trunks look when there's been rain. That rain will soak through to me. Insects will burrow endlessly, above and around me. They'll tunnel across the tip of my nose. The groundskeeper's mower will rumble my earthen walls, and when he's done, flying insects will settle again and resume their preening. I'll have Garfield beside me to natter at. *Did you hear that?* I'll ask him, but I doubt he'll have imagined eternity as anything like lying on a picnic blanket with me on a perfect summer day. He'll only say, *Please stop talking, Margaret. You're dead.*

Melissa is here with me now, standing, perhaps, on the very spot. Both of us know, but of course neither will say, that the next time Melissa stands here it will likely be to see me into the ground. Does it help to practice for such a thing? To bring your own granddaughter to a dress rehearsal like this? We can't ever tell Joanne we've been here, and I don't even want to tell Lee. Melissa can tell them later, if she's of a mind. What I want to say to Melissa is that it's one thing to plan ahead, and another entirely to know precisely where you'll spend eternity, and with whom. There should be an element of surprise. Nothing quite so bold as believing that you can hold death off indefinitely as long as you haven't made those final plans, but rather that where you lie, whether burned to ash or pickled and still looking more or less like yourself, isn't the thing that matters.

I do business when I come out here, too, and it's a nuisance, having to stop by and see everyone. Still here, are you? I want to say, and I think I may have said it once out loud and upset Joanne. It's ridiculous, paying calls like this, weeding your husband and your mother-in-law, telling them both all the things you wanted to say when they were alive, ripping at the grass the mower leaves around the stone, flicking fallen leaves off its face.

Melissa asks me where Lillian is, and I point. Over there, under that oak, I say. The one with the knobby trunk that always puts me in mind of the way Lillian's ankles swelled out over the tops of her black shoes. I say I'm too tired and send her over alone. I never knew Gar's father, and I don't fancy visiting Lillian on the off chance that she's had the same idea about eternity as I have and is lying there chuckling because she knows I'm coming soon, because she's planning to natter at me for all time to come.

It was Melissa's idea to drive out here. I don't know that I would have thought of it. It's all right coming here with her, at least she asked first. Joanne has a habit of altering the route while driving home and then just turning into the cemetery with no warning whatsoever. She leads you over to whichever grave it is she's decided to be penitent over, and cries silently with her head bowed and her hands clasped, and you leave when she wants to leave, no matter how you feel about it yourself. There's just one letter's difference between interred and interned. I thought that one up one day when I was here with Joanne.

I tell Missy I want to go to the cemetery in Ft. Madison next. We've been over this road a thousand times together, she and I, but never with her driving. I have eighteen miles to think about whether I want to drive past the old houses while we're there. If we park on Avenue F across the street from Porter and Frances's house, she will tell me about the time she was right there, playing in the yard, waiting to be called for dinner, when the paper boy had hit her square in the head with the evening paper. She'll tell me that he kept riding but yelled, You okay? over his shoulder, and that she nodded as he receded and she was left standing there, rubbing her head. She will tell me this, forgetting that she told me once before, not knowing that I saw the whole thing but never said, that I'd only gone to the window to check on her and then stayed to see whether she cried or if she went back to playing. And if I could turn around from that window now, Porter and Stephen would be there behind me. Porter would be laughing and Stephen would be lighting his pipe and smiling, pleased that he'd made Porter laugh. Joanne and Lee would be in the kitchen helping Frances get the supper on the table, forgetting themselves entirely and getting along just fine. Joanne was never so much at ease as when we were with Frances and Porter, and whenever Joanne loosened her grip, the rest of us could breathe out as well. It's a wonder we didn't just move in.

But I don't want to park in front of all of the places I used to live, even if that means I can't show them to Melissa myself. There's no point in looking when I'm the only one left who remembers opening those doors, calling hello, and hearing the voices of my family, of everyone who was born and died ahead of me, calling hello back. The cemetery will be all I can take. I'm already having trouble, watching out the car window while we cover this familiar road at fifty-five miles per hour. There's no one behind or in front of us. I want to tell Melissa to slow down, tell her that it's all happening too fast. Is this the last time I'll be on this highway? If it is, then I'm glad that it's Missy I'm with, Missy I'm going the rounds of the cemeteries with. Joanne would want to know where the flowers were, if I had brought along any wreaths, and then she'd cry at the lack of wreaths, and at my lack of feeling. Melissa will just drive where I tell her to drive, and walk me back to the car when we're done. If she asks questions, that's fine, but I don't imagine that she will. She remembers some of these people a little; she never knew the others. There will be other graves for her to stand over when she's as old as I am.

Porter is first, and I surprise myself and laugh a little once I'm standing there. Melissa wants to know what's funny, and I tell her that, by rights, we should head for the cemetery in Denver next, to say hello to Estelle and Harry. But then we're both quiet, because Melissa remembers Porter and Frances. I ask Missy if she remembers Porter's habit of crouching whenever she had something she wanted to say to him, the way he sat on his heels so he wouldn't be taller than she was, the way he always sat on the floor with her at Christmas to see her new toys, and she nods.

I feel mutinous suddenly, even angry. How could I never have realized before that I could be buried here? Ashes to ashes, Doud to Doud. It's burial with family, either way, and how would that be more sad than Estelle and Harry's being buried a thousand miles away in Denver without any of the rest of us? I shake my head to dispel the thought as soon as I've had it. Joanne would never allow it. A plot, my plot next to Garfield, has been waiting for me for thirty-five years. I wrote the check myself, put the deed in my safe deposit box, and she knows it. Still, I can't entirely banish the notion, because it feels like something more than devilry. It's not Garfield I mind so much as being buried with both him and his parents. It's too dynastic. I'm no Ruth, and Lillian was no Naomi. I tell myself to forget it, that graves are only for the living. The dead don't need reminding where they've left themselves.

I look at Melissa and I wonder what she would make of all of this. She has my old habit of saying nothing in response to her mother, so it's anyone's guess what she's actually thinking at any given moment. I've always imagined her as my ally, of course, or my hope. The version of myself who will get it right and break free of all of this. A person might think that a mother would see everything she needed to see in her own daughters' faces, but there was more for me to see, and it's here in Melissa. She looks like me. More than Joanne or Lee ever did, and I wonder how that happens. How a set of features and even gestures can hop a generation like that.

Over here, I tell her, and I point to where we're going next, because I've just realized why I wanted to do this, why I wanted to spend this morning alone with Melissa among these graves. To go the rounds with her, of course, and say hello or good-bye or whatever it is that you say when you're visiting a place on your own steam for the last time, when you suspect that the next time you're here you'll have arrived feet first. But more than that, I want to tell her about the ring box. I have to tell her. It's not so far from Porter's plot to Mother and Dad's, and I'm working out how I will say it, how I will get the words out because I'm crying already. We're crossing the frozen ground and I'm holding her arm tighter and tighter and I'm gulping, trying to get air, trying to control my voice so I can tell her about the ring box I buried in my mother's grave nearly fifty years ago and what I put inside.

·—*33*—·

ELEGIE

A brick house set back from the street
Embraced by clinging ivy
A birdhouse painted in a way the birds don't like
    but men do
People come here to unburden themselves of their
    troubles
A man gives advice, and people prosper in follow-
    ing it
Children play outside the house
God love them, the man says, and turns away again
    to help his fellow man
The door opens to a young girl dressed in white
The man gazes fondly on the girl
This is my daughter, he says to his fellow man
When the great man's work is done, night falls and
    his family sleeps
Morning comes, and the great man feels ill
His daughter tries to help him, but the Angel of
    Death has entered
The family gathers
The casket is closed, and the great man sleeps

J found the poem on Joanne's nightstand the week after Garfield died. She'd written it on a piece of notebook paper and left it there, folded it up. I likely shouldn't have read it, and have never admitted to her that I did. I copied it out, though, and hid it in my dresser drawer, laid flat under the lining paper.

It enraged me when I first read it, but what angered me thirty-five years ago only saddens me now. The way she elevated Garfield and herself, the way she all but left out Lee and me. The way she absolved herself, dressed in white, a child doing battle with the Angel of Death. I'm throwing my copy of the poem out; I don't want her to find it after I'm gone. It would only call attention to the absence of a comparable poem for me. I don't want one anymore, though. I understand now that to be taken so thoroughly for granted, to be depended upon to live a long life was my unthought-of goal all along. I never wanted veneration, only respect.

The Great Man. How that would have pleased him. But as soon as I've thought that much, distaste bubbles up and I'm provoked into imagining that the next thing he'd have pointed out was the way she misspelled Elegy in the title, and wouldn't she prefer to copy it out fresh?

I know the truth of this poem. I know that Garfield was as capable of giving excellent advice as he was incapable of hearing it for himself. Nothing pleased him more than being asked his opinion, and there was true generosity in the way he doled out wisdom. It was wisdom after all that prompted him to surround Tonty Dunne with her own flowers when she lay dying. It rankles, though, that I can hardly remember the good. Aside from Joanne, there was no one in the family who would have described Gar as his friends would have done. I resented his being two people at once, and the way he squandered his kindness on strangers.

I wonder what Garfield would make of this, what he would say if he were the one telling it instead of me. Cry fair or foul, or even laugh? Remind me that even if our souls did not connect, our bodies certainly had. Wink slowly and say, I took you away from nothing and no one, Margaret. You had already chosen nothing over Byron when I first looked at you. You looked back when you could have looked away. And that was that.

He might claim that I'd been the disappointment. He might say that he'd been waiting for me to put up a better fight, and claim it so credibly that I'd be propelled toward doubt. And knowing all that he knows now in the hereafter, he might even say that he'd never really been cruel, only insecure and fearful. He might reasonably point out that he'd only done what was expected of him, that, by rights, if he was the family's head, he should have done all of our thinking for us. That we'd both been hamstrung by the times in which we had lived.

I never met Gar's father, but I freely admit that he bettered him in one thing at least: in believing that his daughters should be fully educated, Garfield insisted on their worth. If he was sorry we never had sons, he never said so, nor did he ever imply that he had deserved a prettier wife.

Look at that. I said something nice and I meant it.

I had been sure by the time I met Garfield that I'd learned everything I needed to know to make my choice. I knew, even if I didn't fully understand it, that I could trust that Garfield saw in me something that was absent in the other women he had met. I knew that people around me were startled when I bagged an attractive, charismatic man, just as they had to concede Garfield's hidden depths when they saw me on his arm. And later, when I learned that an uneducated woman and a domineering man didn't always square, I had also learned that much of what happened each day could be forgiven in the bedroom at night.

If you can sometimes know a thing without proof or experience, then you can know a person without ever having met. Something in me made it possible for Garfield Maguire to look at me as if he already knew me. And it seemed to me, when I first looked at him, that he was the reason I'd gotten up and gotten dressed that day, that everything had led to my standing at that pleasant party, forgetting what I'd just been saying and to whom, because the grinning man with the black pomaded hair was coming toward me, his hand reaching out for mine.

·—34—·

J've spooned the broth out of my bowl, but left the chicken and vegetables. I put one more oyster cracker on my tongue to mollify Melissa, but she's giving me that same disappointed scowl.

You couldn't keep a bird alive on what you're eating, Damma.

Probably a good thing I'm not a bird, then, I say.

We both know it's the next report to Joanne that's got her worried while she's busy policing my dinner. The number of crackers I did or did not eat, the success with which I've visited the toilet. The phone table is right there in the hall outside my bedroom door, and the phone itself is on a short cord. There's no way to drag it around the corner, no second jack at the other end of the house to plug it into. I can hear everything Melissa says, of course, and most times I can hear Joanne, too, on the other end.

She's only scared, I'd like to tell Melissa. She's not really angry. Joanne's hardly ever been truly angry in all her life, she's been too busy being afraid. Still, this snowstorm is worrying, and that will be hard on Melissa. It's sure to drive Joanne to fever pitch. She'll be unbearably shrill.

If I had my druthers, Melissa would talk back. I saw her do it once when she was twelve or so and lying with her markers spread out on my living room carpet, coloring in the letters on the garage sale sign she was making for me. Joanne, the corporate art director, wanted to know why she'd drawn bubble letters. Shouldn't she stick to the darker colors, and forget the yellow? Why hadn't she left room for an exclamation point, and shouldn't she draw a big black arrow at the bottom, pointing the way?

A laugh like a dog's bark tore out of me when Melissa looked up with the yellow marker in her hand and said with undisguised irritation, Do you want to do it?

It shut her mother up, and the fact that I had laughed made it impossible for Joanne to scold her. Still, I doubt she ever tried it again. The element of surprise was lost, and when puberty hit Melissa soon after, it took the wind right out of her. Her shoulders slumped in defeat, and she didn't smile or even really look at you in photos for years.

I think this snowstorm's got us trapped here in the house, or at least it soon will have. I told Melissa to turn off the radio a while ago, because the weather report seemed to be on repeat. Snowbound is the word I want, but I don't want to talk about snow at all. Melissa looked panicked enough when I admitted I felt faint and wanted her to help me into bed. She doesn't need reminding that there's a blizzard outside. Still, it's almost dark out, and I'd like to watch it snowing. I'll ask Melissa to open the curtains soon, and she can sit with me or not in the dark, as she chooses.

When the phone rings, it comes as an odd sort of relief. The clock resets each time Joanne calls, and ratchets the tension down a few notches so it can start building again, fresh. No one is ever quite as worried as Joanne, no one's nerves are quite as frayed. The rest of us are simply thoughtless; too busy with our own navels to consider her, but it never does to call her on it because the only thing worse than Joanne in a fury is Joanne in tears.

Melissa's got the receiver out an inch at least from her ear, whether because of her mother's squawking or to let me hear better, I don't know.

Get her to the hospital, Joanne is saying. I don't know what you're still doing at the house.

She doesn't want to go.

She doesn't get to vote.

Does her doctor get to vote? Melissa says, and I nod *good girl*. He says she's probably just as well off resting here tonight, and if anything changes, I can bring her in.

Melissa holds the receiver still farther from her ear. She rolls her eyes at me, *here we go*, but she crosses her legs and her foot starts bouncing midair like she'd rather kick something.

If anything changes, you call an ambulance. Don't mess around with your car. And don't wait for her to tell you something is wrong.

How am I supposed to know what's wrong before she tells me?

Just watch her, Melissa. Joanne raps out the words like she's got a half-wit on the line. Melissa's foot stops and she stares at a spot on the floor.

Melissa?

Yes, Mother.

I hope you're listening to the radio. It's supposed to snow all night across three states. I'm snowbound, and you're going to be snowbound, too. I won't be able to get there before tomorrow at least, and I've told Lee to stay home. Is the driveway clear?

It will be.

It had better be. I'm relying on you.

I'd heard Garfield a thousand times talking to Joanne that way, with his voice raised like an angry hand, and she had always let herself be cowed, even as she was silently baffled by the scolding. I thought my heart would break the first time I heard Joanne aim Garfield's voice at Melissa, but Melissa has only ever allowed it to deflate her part way, almost from the time she could talk, so that even at the age of three or so when she had dribbled her way to the bathroom and left a trail of yellow dots in the hall, she met Joanne, towering above her, with defiance.

If you can't control yourself, I can put a litter box in your bedroom! Joanne raged, and Melissa, though she couldn't stop herself from crying, answered, I am not an animal. I can see that she's deflated now, more than she should be, and when she hangs up the phone I tell her, Just leave it. My plowing service will come in the morning, and by then the city will have cleared the streets.

It's going to snow all night, she says.

You can't shovel all night, I tell her.

Melissa exhales and smiles a little. Actually, yes, she says, I can. We might need to get you to the hospital before morning.

I'm not going to any hospital tonight.

Damma—

No. Now listen to me, Melissa. You listen to me. I will not be carried through the snow to the hospital, and I'm glad it's you here tonight instead of your mother. I believe you'll respect my wishes. Of course, I say this more out of hope than real conviction, and hope she'll miss the difference in my voice. No, now Missy, don't look like that. I'm not planning on dying just yet.

She's standing at the end of the bed and glowering at me now, but I just glower right back.

Then you won't mind if I keep the drive clear, anyway, she says.

You're a grown woman. If you want to spend the night shoveling snow, that's your business. At least that'll keep you from hovering over me.

No, it won't. I've promised to watch you, too.

How am I going to get any sleep with you scraping outside with the shovel and stomping around in your boots?

I'll keep quiet. Now, quit complaining, or I'll give you a shovel and put you to work.

I laugh at that. I like it when she sasses me, and she knows it. I used to sass my father to rile Estelle, who never quite got the hang of reading his eyes, never knew for certain if I'd finally annoyed him or not. Funny that a thing like that would jump a generation, too.

I stop her before she's through the door. I mean it, Melissa. She turns to look at me again, and gives me a nod.

It's comforting, at first, to listen to Melissa outside. But then it puts me in mind of Garfield doing the same thing, our first winter in this house, when shoveling our own driveway was as novel for him as watching him do it was for me. I'd seen him shovel Lillian's drive many times, and I'd shoveled her drive myself during the war, but there was no charm in that, it was just a job to be done. Our driveway here was long, at least double the length of Lillian's, and Garfield had a way of standing at the top and looking straight down to the street before he started, just leaning on the shovel and taking it all in in a proprietary sort of way. Then, when he got to the bottom, he'd do the same thing from there and look back up the whole tidy length of it toward the house and the garage.

I used to open the drapes and watch him when he shoveled at night. I'd pull the ottoman over and sit there in the front of the picture window with an afghan around me while the snow accumulated on the trees and the yew hedges and swirled in the light around the post lamp. The girls were asleep and the house was quiet, except when the furnace cycled on, and Gar would turn and wave to me when he reached the bottom of the drive. He was a solid man and his movements were compact somehow, precise. Watching him like that put me in mind of the time before we were even sweethearts, when I always seemed to be looking at him from a distance. He shoveled without pausing, out of vanity I thought, because he knew I was watching. It's always Garfield I'm watching in these memories. The air is always still, there is never any wind, the snow increasing on the branches grows impossibly high, and the blanket of snow on the yard in the mornings that follow is always glittering and brittle.

Melissa comes in to sit when she's done. She switches off my lamp without asking and opens the curtains on the window over-looking the yard.

Is it letting up? I say.

No. It's pretty though. Here, sit up so you can see.

Oh, I don't need to see out, I say. I do enough of that from here already. But I let her lift me all the same and stack the pil-lows up behind my back. It looks just as I'd imagined it would, the only thing missing is the silhouette of a man at the bottom of the drive.

You all right? she says.

I can't tell her what I'm thinking, so I just nod my head and lean back into my pillows. The window throws the post lamp's light in rectangles across my coverlet.

I wanted to live on a farm, I say.

Melissa answers me without surprise, as if we'd been talking about farms all along. I didn't know that, she says.

A big farm, I say. Not with livestock, just corn and beans. We lived near farmland when I was a girl, and I used to sneak off to the fields when I should have been home, helping Mother. She always gave me an earful when I finally slunk home, but I'd go off just the same the next day and come home with wildflowers in my pockets and anthers in my hair, so there was no disguising where I'd been.

And then when we were in high school, I'd drag Estelle out in Dad's car on summer nights to listen to the corn. She belly-ached about it, of course. She had better things to do, she said, and anyone who believed that corn made noise belonged in the sanatorium up on the hill, but then once I got her out there, she was always quiet. She'd lean against the car with me and listen. You wouldn't believe there was an insect left in the world that wasn't in those fields, and if you kept real still, and kept still long enough, you'd swear you could hear the corn grow.

I could have kept Melissa there quite a while, running off the list of things I'd wanted and never got. Or didn't want until it was too late, didn't know I wanted, or should have wanted but never quite got around to. A dining room. That has always provoked me, the lack of a dining room in this house, and so it sits at the top of the list. Not because it's most important. There are more important things than the annoyance you feel each Thanksgiving and Christmas when you haul the folding tables in from the garage and wipe the legs clean of the same dead spiders and their same exhausted webs and then set them end-to-end in the living room with your wedding linen and china on top as if it's mahogany underneath, or even just oak.

How I'd like to go back and startle Garfield with a tap on the shoulder, make him jump right where he's sitting at his mother's kitchen table, point at those cherished house plans that he's got all spread out and tell him that he'll be dead in six years, so couldn't he just save us all some trouble and rent an office downtown and let me have that space there for a dining room? And while we're at it, that magnolia he's marked out there in the front yard will be just as messy every spring as the crab apple I want in that spot, and his pear tree, too. He should rethink that, because I'm here to tell you the fruit will always be useless and a godawful mess besides.

That one makes me laugh, and Melissa wants to know what I'm thinking. I consider telling her, but decide not to confuse the issue, and go back to where I left off with Dad's car in the road instead.

I say, One of the nights I dragged Estelle out, she didn't want to go because she'd heard thunder off in the distance and thought it was going to rain. Well, I'd heard the thunder, too, but I made like I hadn't, and put her in the car, anyway. We were parked and standing in the road when the sky let loose. Estelle went shrieking her head off and got back in the car, but I stood there and laughed at her, pounding on the window from inside the car to get my attention. I had left the headlights on because there was no moon that night and I'd known it was going to rain, and I danced on the road in the light in front of the car, and twirled and spun in the mud I made, and I think I may have even howled.

And then what happened?

I got older. We moved to Dalton and Dad sent me to secretarial college, and after that I met Garfield.

No, I mean that night.

Oh, land, I don't remember. I suppose I got us scolded.

I can tell Melissa wants more. I don't usually talk this way, and I think she'd listen to me all night. But I'm tired now. I'm always tired. Even just sitting up in bed and thinking like this wears me out.

Help me with these pillows, I say, and Melissa takes away all but one pillow till I'm lying flat again. She starts to close the curtains again, but I stop her. No, leave it, I say. I'll be awake later and I'll need something to look at.

She's on her way out the door, closing it behind her, and I stop her one more time.

Melissa?

Yes, Damma?

I want to tell her not to be afraid. That her life will change, that everything will change and change again and it will seem sometimes that she is adrift, but she won't be. I want to tell her that she is everything I could have wished to be, but I can't look at her and manage to say that, so I look back out the window.

Don't neglect the things you want, I say instead.

·—35—·

*W*hen I was little, I would crawl under the porch of our house and watch people go by, sometimes for hours, it seemed. There was a loose piece of lattice at the end of the porch that I could crawl in by and then push back in place to disguise the fact that I was there. I kept a piece of cardboard to kneel on, so I wouldn't get too dirty and make Mother ask me where I'd been. We lived on a busy corner, and there were plenty of shoes going by. Dirty shoes and well-kept ones, shoes in a hurry and shoes taking their time. There were even bare feet sometimes, but those were children, some of them smaller than I was, and although she never said so, Mother didn't like for us to play with children whose families didn't shoe them when every horse in town was shod.

I liked the shade down there on hot days, and I preferred the pill bugs to Estelle, who tended to ignore me and read, stretched out on the blue rag rug in our bedroom. I could watch Porter come and go, too. I'd hear him running through the house first, down the stairs and out the door with Mother yelling, Walk! behind him. Sometimes he'd slow down enough to catch the screen before it went crack in its frame, and sometimes not, and then he'd launch himself off the porch and take off running in the grass to wherever it was he was running that day. He knew where to find me when he wanted company because I'd shown him the loose lattice and taken him under the porch with me one day. Or maybe he'd known about it first and had been the one to show me. In any case, he didn't like being down there. He didn't fit, he was just too tall, and anyway he said he preferred the open air. Sometimes he'd barely pause after he'd jumped past the porch steps, he'd just look back and wave at me. C'mon, he'd say, and I'd scramble out and wonder where we were going that day. The frog pond, the corn fields further along the road out of town, or even the depot, where the grown-ups were happy to say hello because they knew us and knew we could be trusted to not get in the way.

It wasn't all that swell being under the porch, but I did like the shade and I liked having something of my own. I suppose I liked to pretend that I knew things that others didn't, too, and I kept pretty fair track of our neighbors' comings and goings. If I was still there when Dad got home, I'd wait until he'd walked over my head and into the house before I came out, and then I'd brush my knees clean and go in after him and we'd both pretend he hadn't seen me there when he came up the walk, so he could tease me and ask me how my day at work had been, since I was getting home even later than he did. Mother called me to come in sometimes, always from the kitchen door, and I'd run around the back of the house so she wouldn't guess I'd been at the front the whole time. If she wanted me for a chore she'd yell, Maggie! Maggie Doud! But if she just wanted my company at the sink or the stove she'd call, Maggie Peggy Magpie! and watch for me to come running with a hand on her hip and the other held up to shade her eyes. She'd slap my braids on my shoulders and tell me, Giddap! and I never once suspected she'd known where I was the whole time.

She's made me a cake, she tells me, but I'm not allowed to see until after supper, and she kisses the top of my head and swats me in the direction of the bathroom so I can wash. And when she calls us all to supper, I remember my napkin and put it in my lap before I'm told and she winks at me. Dad fills my plate, and it's all my favorites. Pork roast, green beans, and mashed turnips. Mother has the lace cloth on the table and the little wineglasses for the grown-ups. And there are two of Mother because Aunt Ada is there, but that's all right, even though they never miss a chance to remind me that the sight of the two of them together made me cry when I was a baby. I'm excused from helping to clear because it's my birthday, and Mother waits to come back until they've turned out the lights and I see her face above the candles on the cake and everyone is singing.

I count the candles and I am five. It's not really dark inside because it's summer and it's only suppertime, and when I've blown the candles out I can still see the same. Mother is handing around plates of cake and someone asks if we can take them out on the porch and when she says, Yes, our chairs all scrape back on the floor and she cries, Walk! because we've all got her good china in our hands. I know they'll want to sit out there until dark and we children can sit on the steps until the fireflies come out. I'd like to catch some and watch them light inside my cupped hands. I'll show Estelle, because she likes to see too, but she's a ninny and she sits on her hands and won't believe us when we say that they don't bite.

Mother is leaning over me and I ask if I may go outside now. She's smiling at me, asking me if I'd like some water and I take a sip from the straw she's got coming out of the glass, but then I sputter and get water on my chin. She pats me dry with a napkin and I thank her. She's smiling at me, she's calling me Damma and telling me that she's Melissa, she's Missy, and I look at her and wonder how I could have gotten that wrong.

Her smile is turning into something else now. She's searching my face, seeing something new. She's hardly blinking. She looks older suddenly, awed and tender. I think I can see how she'll look in another ten years or so. How she'll look when she has children of her own.

I could tell Missy that I was just with Mother, but I suspect she already knows. I don't want to say anything out loud right now. I don't want to do anything that might keep Mother from coming back again. She'll find me. She'll know me, even though I'm old. She'll know that I'm Maggie. I'm Maggie Doud.

ACKNOWLEDGMENTS

I OWE thanks to many people, first among them my father, who was my first and best writing teacher, and my husband and our daughters, who love and support me every day.

I thank the members of my MFA writing group, Elisabeth Fairfield Stokes, Michelle Hoover, Michelle Valois, Jane Rosenberg LaForge, and Patricia Horvath, who remember that this novel began life as a short story, and who remain my dear friends today.

Thanks to my agent, Melanie Jackson, and my editor, Jill Bialosky, for their intelligence, enthusiasm, and dedication.

And finally, my deep thanks to family and friends who have supported me in countless ways: Patricia McArdle, Christy Lorgen, Jay Neugeboren, Holly Robinson, Kent Carroll, Rosalind Morris, Teresita Alvarez-Bjelland, Masha Strømme, Ian Cooper, Emma Prunty, and Ida Eliassen-Coker.